SICILIAN DEFENSE

BOOKS BY JOHN NICHOLAS IANNUZZI

FICTION

Condemned
J.T.
Courthouse
Sicilian Defense
Part 35
What's Happening?

NON-FICTION

Handbook of Trial Strategies
Handbook of Cross Examination
Trial: Strategy and Psychology
Cross Examination: The Mosaic Art

SICILIAN DEFENSE

A NOVEL

JOHN NICHOLAS IANNUZZI

A MADCAN BOOK

ISBN 978-1-4804-7679-0

Cover image, *New York Cityscape*, by Kurt Schumann

Cover design by Neil Alexander Heacox

Distributed Open Road Distribution
345 Hudson Street
New York, NY 10014
www.openroadmedia.com

To Geri

SICILIAN DEFENSE

MONDAY, FEBRUARY 8

11:15 P.M.

ICY WIND LASHED THE CONSTANT RAIN; beams of light from the streetlamps slithered across the deserted sidewalks of Mulberry Street. Cars huddled at the curbs. From the brick tenements above, life glimmered through frost edged windows.

A white neon sign flickered TWO STEPS DOWN INN through the plate-glass front of the small restaurant in the middle of the block.

Within, lights were shining brightly; several men sat at tables near the front. The jukebox pulsed with the tones of Sergio Franchi's *Male Femmina*. Franchi dominated all the jukeboxes since Jimmy Rosselli had become temperamental about appearing at the Italian Civil Rights League concert.

The restaurant had fifteen white-clothed tables in front. Toward the rear, behind a small divider, were a few more tables, a television set hung from the ceiling, and a glass-faced refrigerator, its shelves filled with wine, fruit, vegetables and whipped-cream pastries. Further back was a small service bar and, through a passage, the kitchen.

"Hey, Mike," called one of the men sitting in front, "turn off the jukebox and let's have the news." This was Gus, about forty-five, thin, balding and tough-looking.

Mike, the owner of the restaurant, walked forward, stood on a chair and tuned the TV, then moved to the jukebox, cutting Franchi in midnote.

"Shepard and the other astronauts are on the way back, aren't they?" asked Angie the Kid. He was at Gus's table. Angie was young, dark-haired, tall and very strong. He was just learning the ropes that, he hoped, would help him to earn a living later on. He drove some of the older men, most often Gus, around town, ran errands and wanted much to belong. Angie the Kid's greatest asset at the moment was that he had a lot of heart, which meant he didn't step back from a fight, and could take it as well as give it.

"Tomorrow's the splashdown," said Bobby Matteawan. He sat alone. "You know, it rains every time they go to the moon. It rained three days the first time. It's been raining two days now already." Bobby Matteawan was about forty, short, dark, thick-necked and thick-bodied. His family name was actually Vinci, but the name by which everyone knew him had been derived from the State Hospital for the Criminally Insane where he had spent an unpleasant five years. In all, Bobby Matteawan had spent sixteen of his first twenty-eight years in various state institutions reserved exclusively for criminals. Since then he had been clean of police trouble. Bobby Matteawan had something other than heart—when aroused, he was an uncontrollable fury.

The front door opened. The angry wind forced its way into the restaurant as Tony Mastropieri came in. Tony, small and thin, had no nickname. He was known only as Tony, but people around town knew who was meant when someone mentioned Tony. Those who didn't know got the vibrations of his awesome reputation just by looking at him—at the thin lips that never smiled, the dark steely eyes that never wavered. Tony unbuckled his long leather coat. Beneath it, he was dapper in a dark suit and shirt and pale silk tie. He and Louie the Animal, his driver, had just finished snaking their way across Manhattan, picking up the weekly take from the bookies, numbers men, and shylocks for Sal Angeletti.

"Hiya, Tony," said Angie the Kid. The others nodded absently, still absorbed in the space mission.

"Where's Sal?" asked Tony, looking toward the empty table behind the divider where Sal usually held business meetings or settled dis-putes throughout the afternoon and evening.

"He hasn't been in all night," replied Bobby Matteawan.

"Where's Joey—he should know," suggested Tony. He took a nap-kin and wiped his shoes.

"He just went over to Sal's house to check."

Sal Angeletti was, not in the ordinary sense, a banker. He supplied money to the smaller lights in the underworld cosmos for a percentage of interest called "vig." Sal didn't take bets or numbers, didn't even have runners or controllers working for him. That was small potatoes. Sal was a money man, a banker's banker who, like J. P. Morgan, dealt only with professionals. Since Sal knew the people he dealt with, and they in turn—only too well reminded by his collectors—knew who they were dealing with, his risk was small and he could therefore charge an interest rate of just 1 or 2 percent a week. The money men in the street, dealing with such high risks as gamblers and people in a bind, charged a higher vig—3-5 percent a week. As the collections were made each week, Sal would wheel the money, that is, like a bank, put it out' again in the street, earning interest on the interest. Sal had five top men, or lieutenants. The second in command was Frank Grossi, called Frankie the Pig. Then came Joey, who was closest to Sal, then Tony, Gus, and Bobby Matteawan. All were assigned certain areas in which to make weekly collections, all earned 10% of their weekly takes; none was ever arrested, nor did their names appear in the newspapers—that was for hoods involved in violent and large-scale crime.

In addition to collecting for Sal, the five lieutenants each had men of their own to direct and control, and each had invested their money in legitimate acivities. Gus operated B-girl bars in the mid-forties for tourists who wandered off the beaten path from Times Square. Bobby Matteawan had fag joints in the Village. Tony and Joey were more unattached in their operations; they had interests in trucking and other ventures.

A couple of men entered the restaurant and looked toward the empty table in the back.

Gus recognized them as some of Sal's friends from uptown. "He's not here right now. You want me to tell him something?"

"We'll come back," said the shorter man. "We're going over to the Grotto for some linguini. Is Frankie the Pig around?"

"No, he probably won't be back tonight."

The two men left the restaurant.

"Where's Frankie, with *a cummad'*?" asked Tony. He ordered an espresso with anisette.

"Where else?" Gus laughed. "When he gets involved with a new *cummad'*, that's the end of him—he bangs himself out for two weeks, then he's ready to come around again."

Frankie the Pig was six-foot-two-inches tall, 275 pounds heavy, and he had plenty of strength and heart, cunning and viciousness. He had plenty of temper, too. Everybody feared Frankie.

"Who's he with now?" Tony continued.

"Some dame from the West Side, an *Irish fidend*," replied Bobby Matteawan.

Tony made a face. "What good is a bony, cold *cummad'* you've got to get drunk to bang?"

They laughed and turned their attention to the television again.

"I wish they'd give the track results," said Gus. "It's too cold to go to 14th Street for the papers."

"You dopey bastard, I bet you'd walk through snow up to your ass to see if your lousy horses came in," said Tony.

Gus shrugged. "Frankie's got his *cummadas* and I've got my horses. At least once in a while one of my horses gives me something, like a two-horse parlay or a fifty-dollar winner. What the hell?" Gus was thoughtful for a moment. "If I had all the money I've gambled away . . ."

"You and Sal. Boy, the money he spends at the track is really wild," said Angie the Kid. He looked around with a smile.

"Maybe that's where he's gone," Tony suggested. "Maybe he's up in Yonkers."

"On a night like this? Besides, you know he doesn't go without Joey."

The door opened. Joey walked in. He was the youngest of Sal's lieutenants, tall, trim and dark-haired. He shook his head. "He isn't there. I don't know where he could be. His wife doesn't know either. She started to get worried, but I told her I just missed him somewhere else, and I'd meet him here."

"Where the hell can he be?" Gus began to get agitated. "When did you see him last?"

"This afternoon," said Joey. "He wanted me to do something for him and told me not to pick him up afterward."

"What time was that?" asked Tony.

"About five-thirty."

"I can't figure it out," said Joey. It isn't like Sal to go off and not tell anybody where he is. Especially me."

They fell silent. In the background the TV weatherman was predicting continued rain and cold.

As they sat, a car was heard approaching very fast. No one paid it any attention, but the rising drone as the car sped on the wet asphalt crept into the restaurant. Suddenly there was a tremendous sound of crashing metal, as if a car had struck something at high speed. The men whirled around.

"What the hell was that?" Bobby Matteawan snapped. The others rose and looked out. "Holy shit," mumbled Angie the Kid. They all stared incredulously. Tony was the first one into the street.

The body of a man was sprawled on the rear deck of Mike's car, which was parked in front of the restaurant. Blood was dripping onto the white trunk, mixing with the rain, running black over the trunk and down the fenders. They stared at the body, momentarily shocked into inaction. It began to slide on the wet, rounded trunk. No one moved, each fighting the same fear. They couldn't see who it was, because the streetlight was behind the body and blood obscured the head. The corpse slid slowly off the trunk and landed in the gutter; the head bounced off the curb like a slab of beef, with a dull thud, and landed under the rear of the car.

"Jesus Christ," said Joey, springing forward. He knelt and pulled the body, which was lying face down, sliding it from under the car. "Sal, Sal," he called, as he moved the body out and turned it over. He stared, unbelieving, then looked at the faces hovering above him.

"Who the fuck is that?" Tony said, looking into the dead man's face.

"What kind of joke is this?" asked Gus. "I've never seen this guy before."

Mike looked down the street after the car, which had long since disappeared. Up above, people were peering out of their rain-streaked windows. "Hey, the whole neighborhood's watching."

The others looked up. The people in the windows shrank back.

Louie the Animal, who had been outside waiting for Tony, came running through the rain. "Some niggers were just racing up the street holding that guy at the car window—I saw them throw him out. They must have been going a thousand miles an hour when they dumped him."

"And right on my car, the bastards," said Mike.

"Niggers?" Tony asked.

"Those miserable *tutzone* bastards," said Mike, "throwing a stiff in front of my joint."

"We'd better dump him someplace else before the cops think we stretched him," said Gus.

"The guys down at the precinct won't want to find him here either," said Tony.

"Why not push him in front of the next car that comes along," Matteawan proposed, "then we'll call the cops to the accident."

"Are you crazy?" Mike blurted out, before he realized whom he was speaking to.

Bobby turned slowly and stared at him.

"Nothing personal, Bobby," Mike said hastily, "but we can't leave a dead body in front of my place."

"We'll need a car," said Gus.

"Mine's across the street," Joey volunteered.

"Pull it over here, quick," said Tony. "Angie, you drive this stiff over to the piers on the West Side and throw him in the river."

Angie was stunned. "Me?"

"Yes, you. What the hell, if you hang around with us, you've got to get your feet wet sometime," grinned Bobby Matteawan.

"Mike, get some tablecloths or something. I don't want this guy's blood all over my trunk," said Joey.

Angie the Kid looked doubtful. "Somebody ought to go with me," he said, staring at the body in the shadows between the cars.

"Okay, okay. Louie, go with him," said Tony.

Louie the Animal shrugged. He took two tablecloths from Mike, bent down and started to wrap them around the body.

"But everybody's looking," Angie the Kid protested.

"So much the better," said Tony. "Everybody in the neighborhood heard him dumped here. We've got all these witnesses."

"Then why the river? Why not leave him here?"

"Because we don't need the aggravation," said Gus. "Come on, Kid, help Louie wrap up this stiff."

Joey brought his car up beside them.

"Hey, we could put him in the meat grinder in the restaurant and make meatballs out of him," Matteawan chortled. "And with his head we'll make *cappuzell*."

"You crazy bastard," said Tony.

"Mmm, can't you just taste the fatty eyeballs of the *cappuzell*," Matteawan said, rolling his tongue in his cheek.

Angie the Kid looked at him wanly.

"Come on, Kid, help me lift him," said Louie, pulling the body into sitting position. They picked it up and stuffed it into Joey's trunk.

"Don't take too long," said Joey. "He'll bleed through the tablecloths in a few minutes."

"And don't dump the tablecloths with the body," said Tony, "in case they can trace them."

"Okay," said Louie. "You drive, Angie."

Angie hesitated, then reluctantly got behind the wheel.

Just inside the restaurant door the phone in the booth began to ring. Mike went in and picked up the receiver.

"You got that body we left for you?" purred a deep voice with a heavy Southern accent.

"Who's this?"

"Never mind who it is, baby, just listen. We got Sal. You got it, man? We got Sal."

"Who *is* this?" Mike repeated.

"Man, you're not listening. We got Sal."

"Just a minute," said Mike. He dropped the phone. It banged against the wall of the booth as he ran frantically outside. "Listen! There's a guy on the phone. Sounds like a nigger. He says they got Sal."

"What?" Tony ran inside. "Hello?"

"Okay, man, for the last time. We got Sal. And that present we just left for you is to let you know we mean business. Got it?"

Tony gripped the phone until his knuckles turned white. His mouth twisted evilly. "What do you want?"

The others were pressed around him.

"We want to talk to the man in charge now, that's what. Frankie the Pig. We got a message for him. We'll call tomorrow night at eight." The line went dead.

"Hello, hello," said Tony.

There was no answer.

"Son of a bitch. We've really got trouble," said Tony. "They snatched Sal."

Bobby Matteawan let go with a roundhouse left into the side of the telephone booth. The booth shook.

"Take it easy, that's not going to help," said Mike.

"What the hell are we going to do?" asked Joey. "How're we going to find them?"

"We'll kill them," screamed Bobby Matteawan. He punched the wall.

"First we've got to get hold of Frankie the Pig," said Tony. "Who knows where he is?"

They looked at each other, shaking their heads.

"The Kid," Bobby Matteawan remembered, "the Kid drove him over to see that Irish broad before. He knows."

They ran to the door. The car was gone. They saw its tail-lights disappearing around a corner a few blocks down.

"Come on, we've got to catch that kid," said Tony, sprinting toward his car. They jumped in and Tony burned rubber as he pulled away from the curb. The car swayed as it grabbed for traction on the slippery street.

"Where did he go?" asked Bobby.

"He turned left over here," said Tony, spinning through a red light on the corner. About four blocks ahead of them they saw a car turning left toward Canal Street.

"That must be it," said Joey, his eyes straining to see through the rain-splattered windshield.

Tony put his foot to the floor. The car lurched forward. When he got to where the Kid had turned, he put it into a power drift around the corner. The car drifted too much and hit the curb at the bus stop. Tony kept the wheels spinning forward, grinding his way back to the middle of the street. The car ahead made a right onto Canal Street.

"Somebody's following us," said Angie the Kid nervously, looking in the rear-view mirror. Louie the Animal looked back, too late to see anyone behind them. He reached under the seat and took out a pistol that was stuffed into the padding. Angie speeded up and turned right again, now heading uptown on Lafayette.

"The Kid must have spotted the car," said Tony, "but doesn't know it's us."

"Son of a bitch," Joey muttered. "Now he'll drive right past Police Headquarters, and he's speeding, too."

"He can't turn again until he gets to Broome Street," said Tony. "We'll go to Broadway and make a right and then up to Broome. We'll cut him off there."

"Broadway's one-way going downtown," Joey said.

"So what, his license is suspended already—they can't give him a ticket," said Bobby Matteawan.

Tony sped to Broadway, then turned uptown. There was only one car headed downtown toward them. It started to flash its lights to warn them they were going the wrong way.

"Fuck you, Mac," said Tony, flooring the accelerator. The car hurtled to Broome Street, slashed across the intersection with screeching brakes and blocked the street, just as Angie the Kid was about fifty yards from the corner, approaching fast.

Angie swerved and mounted the sidewalk, aiming his car around them. Joey jumped out, right into the oncoming headlights, waving his arms.

Angie, his eyes bulging, his hands locked on the wheel, kept coming. Suddenly a bellow filled the night: "Stop! You dumb Kid!" It was Louie the Animal frantically twisting the wheel. The car came to an abrupt halt.

"Jesus Christ," Louie gasped. He eased out of the car, putting the pistol in his belt.

"It's us," said Tony.

"Yeah, and it almost wasn't," said Louie, looking back into the car. Angie the Kid had his head down on the wheel.

"Don't die now, Kid," said Tony. "You've got to get Frankie the Pig. Get him back to the restaurant right away. Bobby, you and Louie drive this stiff to the river."

"Okay," said Bobby Matteawan. "You're sure you don't want to make a *cappuzell'* out of him?"

"Come on, let's get going," Joey ordered abruptly. "It isn't funny anymore."

TUESDAY, FEBRUARY 9

12:15 A.M.

"THOSE LOUSY FUCKING *tutzones*," said Frankie the Pig, the veins bulging on his massive neck. He was pacing the length of the Two Steps Down Inn. At various tables were seated Tony, measuring Frankie the Pig with his steely eyes; Gus, his feet up on a second chair; Bobby Matteawan, who was sharpening a butcher's cleaver on a honing stone; Angie the Kid, who was watching Bobby Matteawan; Joey and Philly the Splash.

Philly the Splash was an old-timer, gray and thin with age, one of the lieutenants who was no longer very active but who, because he knew the ways of the street, was asked for his counsel. So far, the only thing accomplished was that Frankie the Pig had made Mike nervous, because Frankie was ready to break everything and anything in his way.

"Those lousy niggers, I'll kill them with my own hands," spat Frankie the Pig between clenched teeth. "What did that son of a bitch say? Tell me again."

"Frankie," soothed Philly the Splash, who had got his name by diving off the piers into the East River when he was a kid. In those days, he was the only one in the neighborhood who could swim. "We all know what they said. It's more important to know what we're going to do. That's what we should be talking about." As the old man spoke, his head nodded involuntarily.

Frankie the Pig looked at Philly the Splash, his eyes filled with the strength and anger that made him both feared and vulnerable. "We should find these miserable bastards and kill them," Frankie the Pig said icily.

"I'll go for that," chimed Bobby Matteawan, not looking up from the keen edge of his cleaver.

"I agree," said Philly the Splash. "And where do we find them to kill them? That's the sixty-four dollar question."

Frankie looked out the front window. The rain had washed the blood from the street. "I don't know," he said. "But when we get them, we'll crash them—I can't wait to talk to that guy on the phone tomorrow night."

"You talk like that and they'll kill Sal," warned Philly the Splash.

"Splash is right," said Tony. "First we've got to get Sal back—then we'll worry about getting them."

"If only we had some word from him," said Gus.

"Maybe we should send someone to talk to our friends uptown," Joey suggested. "They might be able to get a line on these niggers for us."

"No," countered Frankie the Pig. "This is something we have to work out ourselves. I mean, how does it look if our boss gets grabbed from under our noses by some niggers?" Frankie looked at them. "We have to figure it out by ourselves, like a matter of honor."

"That's true," said Philly the Splash. "It's something you should work out among the lieutenants."

Suddenly Frankie the Pig picked up a chair and began pulling at the back struts to which the cushioning was attached. His teeth bared as he strained to rip the chair apart.

"For Christ's sake, Frankie," said Mike. "That chair cost me eighteen bucks."

"Then put it on my tab," Frankie grunted as the chair splintered, "before I wreck this whole fucking joint and pay you for nothing."

Mike turned quickly and walked away.

"Anger doesn't accomplish anything," said Philly the Splash. He was silent again. "You know, I was just thinking. I know exactly what would help us. But you may not like the idea—"

"What is it, Splash?" asked Tony.

"I think we could use someone's help."

"A minute ago you agreed we should keep it among ourselves," said Frankie.

"I still think so," said Philly the Splash. "The man I have in mind is a close friend, not just ours but Sal's."

"I think I know who you mean," said Tony. "I think you're right."

"Okay, tell us who it is so we can all get in on it," said Frankie the Pig.

"I'm thinking of Gianni Aquilino."

Suddenly, the restaurant was stone silent. All eyes turned to Frankie the Pig. Angie the Kid was too young to remember. But Tony remembered. Philly the Splash remembered. The older ones all remembered Gianni Aquilino—also known as Gianni Eagle, and later, when his hair had prematurely turned gray, as the Silver Eagle. Formerly the top man in New York, he was the one man whose ideas had helped tame the violent excesses of some of the bloody misfits sprinkled among the peasants who had come to the new world. Those misfits terrorized the nearest people at hand, their own countrymen, just as Negro junkies still prey not upon the rich of Park Avenue, but upon their own brothers.

Not that Gianni Aquilino ran the whole show, or controlled the other mobs. He didn't. He ran his own mob. The others respected him and listened to him, but they kept their own counsel and followed his advice when it suited their own purposes. Thus, when some of the mobs wanted to get in on the lucrative narcotics trade, the Silver Eagle warned against it. In addition to being dirty business, the Silver Eagle cautioned, narcotics were too hot to get involved with. Although other mobs were champing at the bit to deal junk, Gianni's reputation stood in the way.

Some rebels reasoned that if Gianni were dead, they'd be free to pursue their own vices. And if the other bosses refused to agree to kill him, the rebels intended to declare an all-out war in which many would be killed, energies and blood spent profitlessly. The bosses, except for the Silver Eagle, got together and agreed, some very reluctantly, that it would be easier to kill one man—the Silver Eagle, Gianni Aquilino—than to wage a catastrophic war.

It was Frankie the Pig who had been given the contract to kill Gianni Aquilino.

One winter night, twelve years before, he had staked himself outside Gianni's apartment house in the posh upper Fifties. When Gianni came home, Frankie the Pig entered the lobby behind him, drew a pistol and shot Gianni in the head. But Gianni had heard him coming and at the last moment moved just a bit—and the bullet only creased his skull. Gianni was questioned by the D.A. in the hospital—and afterwards, when he was well enough, by the Grand Jury. But Gianni always insisted that he had been mugged by someone he didn't recognize.

While Gianni Aquilino was in the hospital with this bullet wound, another meeting was convened. At this second gathering it was Sal Angeletti who had stood up against the other bosses and argued that Gianni had always been fair—he'd been a stand-up guy and was still a stand-up guy, and he should be allowed to retire as long as he agreed not to have a vendetta. Sal said he would be personally responsible for Gianni. The other bosses reluctantly agreed. And Gianni thereafter retired and went into real estate investments, where he made a formidable and legitimate fortune. Yet the Grand Juries continued to subpoena him anyway, mainly because his elegant presence guaranteed good press coverage.

"What the hell can Gianni do for us that we can't do for ourselves?" said Frankie the Pig finally, breaking the silence. He had been made Sal's underboss because of his undertaking the contract against Gianni. He could see it in his mind as he spoke, back over the twelve years—Gianni standing there and himself sprinting across the lobby, gun in hand. "And besides, you think he'd help us out?"

"You? No. But Sal, sure," said Philly the Splash. "Remember, Gianni owes his life to Sal, and Gianni's always been a stand-up guy."

"I agree. If anybody can help us, he can," said Tony.

"I disagree," said Frankie the Pig.

"Vote on it," said Philly the Splash.

"What vote—what is this, an election?" Frankie the Pig demanded, looking around.

"It's only a suggestion," Philly the Splash returned.

"When Sal's not here, I'm boss," said Frankie, "and I'll decide."

"I don't deny that, Frankie," Philly the Splash said very quietly, taking the stub of the black cigar out of his mouth. He looked directly into Frankie's eyes. "But Sal's life is on the line and we need somebody with a cool head, somebody like Gianni."

"You mean I haven't got a cool head?" Frankie the Pig glared at him balefully.

"Frankie, I was a tough guy too. I may be an old man, but don't try to push me around. I'm just giving you my ideas. If you don't like them, fine. But don't be looking at me like that."

"I don't think you're being cool right now," Tony said to Frankie the Pig.

Frankie turned. Tony's steely eyes met his.

"I bet Gianni would help us," said Joey. "He and Sal have always been like brothers."

"I think it would be a good idea to have someone like Gianni help you with this, Frankie," Philly concluded diplomatically.

Frankie sat and looked at them. He thought for a while, then turned to Philly the Splash. "How can we approach him? Should I call him?"

"No," said Philly the Splash. "Gianni and I are old friends from way back. I think I should ask him to meet me somewhere. He won't come here—Sal wouldn't even want him to."

"Where, then?"

"What about that bar on the West Side, the one by the piers?" said Tony.

"Right, The Other Place," said Philly the Splash. It had been popular with the boys when the longshoremen's unions were being organized. "I'll talk to him alone, and explain the situation. Then if he agrees we can all start figuring this thing out."

"How do we get him to come there?" asked Gus.

"Joey—you can get him to come. Go pick him up and explain it to him," said Frankie the Pig, taking command now that the plan of action had been agreed upon.

"Okay," said Joey. "But it'll take some time. He lives in Pawling."

"Then get going right away," said Frankie. "Drive as fast as you can and meet us over at The Other Place."

2:30 A.M.

The silver Cadillac limousine rolled slowly west on 51st Street toward the Hudson River. From the elevated West Side Highway an occasional car catapulted a spray of water over the retaining walls, splashing down into the streets below. The car stopped at the corner.

"Drive across the street and park under the highway between Fiftieth and Fifty-first," Gianni Aquilino said from the back seat. Joey was sitting next to him.

The car started across the broad avenue beneath the highway. At the edge of the river it stopped. Gianni got out. He was of medium height. His face was handsome, straight-nosed, his hair all gray and wavy. Even though Joey had awakened him in the middle of the night, Gianni, as always, dressed immaculately in a double-breasted suit. He looked around the deserted street. The wind gusted across the river, which here was thick with ice floes between the piers. Even out into the mainstream there was much ice. Gianni hadn't seen the river so frozen for many years. An occasional tug, its running lights aglow, coursed silently past in the dark.

"One of these days, Gianni, I'll be making enough on the books to buy one of these," said Joey, looking admiringly at Gianni's Cadillac.

Gianni smiled. "I know, Joey, I know. I had my fill of days with plenty of cash to hide but not much to spend—unless I wanted the Internal Revenue to jump all over me."

Gianni turned toward The Other Place. The old bar was still frequented mostly by longshoremen during the day. Whenever Gianni or Sal or their friends wanted to meet quietly, without attracting too much attention, this was the perfect place, virtually empty all night.

In the shadows Gianni could see men seated in a car near The

Other Place. He saw another car half a block away with more shadowy figures within it.

Gianni reached into his pocket and took out a thin gold cigarette case. He snapped a matching lighter into life and, with a motion that had become characteristic, he lit the cigarette with one hand while putting the cigarette case back in his pocket with the other. He took a couple of deep puffs, his eyes further scanning the darkness.

He didn't like the looks of it, but if Sal needed him, he had to come. Gianni's hand reached to his right temple, his finger feeling along the ridge of scar tissue left by Frankie the Pig's bullet.

The face of Frankie the Pig appeared before him clearly. So did that dark, wintry night, twelve years earlier when, out of the corner of his eye, he had seen Frankie quickly enter the lobby of his apartment house right behind him.

The doorman was nowhere in sight. Gianni instantly realized what was happening. Frankie the Pig put his hand inside his coat as he started moving across the lobby. Gianni thought to himself: I'm not going to stand here like a clay pigeon. He didn't carry a gun, so he started to sprint toward the mail room and the fire stairway leading down to the cellar. Then he heard a tremendous, echoing explosion. There was a flash of light inside his eyelids, as though, in the dark of the night, the aurora borealis shone white and distant. Only it was hot. And it was horrible pain. Then it faded slowly, becoming dimmer and dimmer.

A siren wailed in the night, as if in some nightmare. Gianni saw a cop sitting beside him, while the siren grew louder and closer.

"What is this?" Gianni asked. "Where are we going?"

"You've been shot, Gianni," said the cop, who wasn't just a dream character. "You're in good shape. Just dug a small hole in your head." The cop's badge shone intermittently, reflecting the passing street lights. His face was a shadow.

Gianni reached up.

"Don't touch it, Mr. Aquilino," said a voice behind him. Gianni tried to look around, but he couldn't move his head.

"That's the Doc," the cop supplied.

"How am I, Doc?" Gianni asked.

"You'll be all right. Just a glancing head wound. Not serious."

"Good thing I've got a hard head." Gianni lay back, trying to laugh.

"Do you know who did it, Gianni?" the cop asked.

"Officer, what sort of people do you think I know? How could I know anyone who would try to mug me?"

The cop smirked and shrugged. "The D.A. 'll be at the hospital. All kinds of brass and everything, Gianni."

The ambulance kept wailing through the street.

"How about leaving me off right here?" Gianni whispered. "Tell them I ran away while we were at a red light. What the hell—I'm the victim. I didn't do anything. Let me buy you a real good hat."

The cop looked at the doctor—the doctor looked away—then up toward the driver. "I can't do that, Gianni," he said reluctantly. "I'd get roasted. Besides, they'll catch up to you later on. You can't go nowhere with your head like that."

"Yes, I guess you're right. Why make it hot for you? I'll go in," said Gianni as he relaxed on the stretcher. "But I can't imagine who did it. Maybe it was some broad in a jealous rage. Wouldn't that be something, at my age. That's what I think I'll tell them—it was some broad in a fit of passion." Gianni laughed. He reached out and quietly handed the cop a bill from his pocket, the first one he touched. It could have been a single or a hundred.

The cop laughed too. He palmed the bill and winked at Gianni.

A heavy cascade of water lifted by a passing car from the overhead highway splattered on the street. Gianni moved quickly out of range and out of his grisly recollection, now walking toward The Other Place. All that past history no longer mattered. Whatever happened tonight would happen. Gianni had little choice of paths. Ordinarily he would have been far more cautious before meeting anyone like this. But Joey was almost Sal's son. If Joey said something for Sal, it was as if Sal spoke. And if Sal spoke, it was as if Gianni's brother spoke.

"Will Sal be here?" Gianni asked. Joey had only told him there was deep trouble and Sal needed him.

"No, he isn't here. That's the trouble. Old Philly the Splash will tell you all about it. We need you desperately. Sal needs you. You know I wouldn't come to you if it was nothing."

As the two men entered the bar, McMahon the bartender looked up.

There were only a couple of old bleary-eyed longshoremen sipping beers at the bar. McMahon nodded toward the back room. Gianni and Joey walked back across the white octagonal-tiled floor. In the light of the revolving Ballantine clock overhead, Gianni saw old Philly the Splash. He looked ancient. Gianni wondered if he looked as old to Philly the Splash.

Philly was smiling. He stood to greet Gianni.

"Hello, Philly," said Gianni. They clasped hands, looking into each other's eyes momentarily. Floods of memories rushed over each of them.

"You look like a million bucks, Gianni," said Philly the Splash. "Like a real movie star. I can see the legit life really agrees with you."

"It's a lot easier than trying to scheme and make scores. It's like a cakewalk." Gianni lit another cigarette.

McMahon walked in and asked, "What will you have?"

"I'll have a coffee," said Gianni. "If you have some anisette, put some in it."

"The same for me," said Philly the Splash.

"I'll wait at the bar," said Joey.

The two men looked at each other, Gianni patient, Philly the Splash pausing a respectful moment.

"The last time I saw you was at a hearing, wasn't it?" asked Philly the Splash. "Have they been bothering you with subpoenas lately?"

Gianni nodded. "They want to keep tabs on me for some reason. I have one for the Crime Commission tomorrow morning." Gianni glanced at his watch. "This morning, as a matter of fact."

"*This* morning?" Philly the Splash looked anxious.

"That's right. If Joey hadn't said it was an absolute emergency, I wouldn't have come."

"It's too bad they still bother a man like you, Gianni," Philly the Splash said, calm again. "After all, you haven't been involved in twelve years; it's a shame."

"They just want me to know they're aware I'm still around—and to remind me that they're still around, I guess," said Gianni. "The real shame is that they purposely wait until I leave for the office in the morning, and then they go to my house to serve the subpoena—they want to upset my wife."

Gianni was eager to hear of the problem that required his presence at two o'clock in the morning, but this preliminary conversation was all part of the protocol. He understood that he was being conciliated by Philly the Splash, who was well aware that Gianni had been not courteously deposed so many years before.

"How is Maria? It's years since I've seen her," said Philly the Splash.

"She's fine, Philly. And so are the kids. Remember little William? He's just finishing law school. And your son, Bobbie? What's he doing?"

"He's with the teamsters. A business agent. He's doing really well."

The two men smiled at each other as McMahon brought the coffee. Although The Other Place was an Irish bar in Hell's Kitchen, Gianni and his friends had always felt at home having their occasional meetings here. Hell's Kitchen had no fewer, perhaps more, murders than anyplace else in the city, but here they were done quietly, without emotion, without fanfare, the bodies sinking softly into the river.

"I'm sorry we had to bother you tonight," Philly started again, "especially since you've got a hearing in the morning."

"That's all right, Philly. I'll stay in town tonight."

They fell silent.

Philly puffed his cigar. Then he squared his shoulders. "Gianni, we have big trouble. Some niggers snatched Sal."

"They *what*?"

"Sal's been kidnaped."

"But why?"

"I don't know. All I know is they dumped a body in front of the Two Steps Down Inn. Some guy nobody knows. A few minutes later, they called and said they've got Sal, and they'll call back at eight o'clock tomorrow night—that's tonight."

"Who are they? Did they ask for ransom?"

"They didn't say anything else. I wasn't there, so I don't know first hand. But we all sat down afterward, and Frankie the Pig—well, you know . . ."

Gianni's eyes studied Philly the Splash as the name floated through the air. Gianni said nothing. He was suddenly aware again of the scar tissue on his right temple.

"Well, he's a hothead," Philly the Splash continued, "and he wants to go out and kill and destroy. Kill who? Destroy what? We don't even know who these people are. And with the blood Frankie the Pig's got in his mouth, he's no good for figuring out those things. So we all thought, since you and Sal have always been so close, that you'd help us—help us get him back. We didn't want to ask people outside our own—it's embarrassing."

Gianni studied Philly silently. After a moment, he said, "What do you want from me?"

"Help us. You were a great man when you were with us, Gianni. You were the top. We need some of that old-time good thinking you have in your head."

"What's the matter with the people you have? Frankie the Pig's a made man. He's a big shot now. Can't he do it?"

Philly the Splash shrugged and raised his eyebrows. "You know that having balls isn't the only thing in this world."

Gianni nodded, pursing his mouth.

"We need your help, Gianni. We all sat down and agreed on it. Frankie the Pig, too. Sal needs you."

"What can I do?"

"Take charge. Help us figure it out. I mean, we haven't a clue. We don't even know where to begin."

"Tell the others to come in out of the cars," Gianni said.

Philly the Splash smiled a craggy, gold-flecked smile and reached over and patted Gianni's arm. "That's why we need you, Gianni, because you're sharp."

Philly the Splash signaled to Joey. Joey walked out to the street. In a few minutes the others entered. Frankie the Pig came in first. Gianni stayed seated. Frankie the Pig looked at the floor, then at the walls, as he walked along the tile floor to the back room. He looked directly at Gianni as he came close to him.

Gianni looked back steadily into the wide face of Frankie the Pig.

"Hello, Gianni," said Frankie. He was subdued.

"Frankie." Gianni was motionless.

The others watched.

Frankie the Pig extended his hand. "We've got to work together, so how about shaking," he said. His hand could almost be heard gliding out, the room was so quiet.

Gianni looked from Frankie's face to the thick hamhock of a hand he offered.

"It's been a long time, Gianni. A lot of things have gone by."

Gianni reached up slowly and grasped Frankie's hand. "Yes, it's been a long time."

"This is Tony," said Philly the Splash, relieved and pleased. Gianni nodded to him. "And this is Gus. You know Bobby Matteawan. And this is Angie the Kid."

Angie the Kid almost tripped over his own feet as he moved forward so Gianni could see him.

"Okay, come on," said Frankie the Pig. "Move the tables and chairs together so we can talk."

The others began to lift upside-down chairs from the tops of the tables, where the sweeper had placed them.

"Things have changed a lot since then," continued Frankie the Pig, sitting next to Gianni. "You know it was something that had to be done."

"And when it was all over, everybody found out narcotics were bad news, and I was right," Gianni said. "But that's ancient history. We have other things to do now."

"Right."

The men had taken seats and were watching Gianni and Frankie the Pig.

"Now, who are we dealing with?" asked Gianni. "Any ideas?"

"The only thing we know is that they're niggers," said Frankie the Pig. "Somebody saw them drop this body in front of the door. And then the guy Tony spoke to on the phone was a *tutzone.*"

"Are you sure of that?" said Gianni.

"He was a nigger all right," said Tony, his dark eyes unmoving. "When I find him, I'll make him turn white with what I do to him."

"All right, we don't have time for that now," said Gianni, looking at them all. "If we're going to accomplish anything, we've got to act constructively, and not worry about the revenge."

"When we get them, I'm going to chop them into little pieces," said Bobby Matteawan.

Gianni stilled Matteawan with his eyes. He turned back to Frankie the Pig. "They didn't ask for money, or say anything else?"

"Nothing. They just said they'd call tonight at eight. They wanted to speak to me."

"They mentioned you by name?" asked Gianni. He nodded thoughtfully. "Where did they call you?" He lit another cigarette, offering his case to the others. Everyone had his own.

"At Mike's restaurant, the Two Steps Down Inn."

"And they'll call there again tonight?"

"I suppose so—they just said they'd call."

"How did they grab Sal?"

"On the way to the restaurant I guess," said Joey. "He sent me on an errand, and said he'd meet me there. He never did."

"They must have the place and everything else pretty well clocked," said Gianni. "Anybody see any colored people hanging around?"

They shook their heads.

Gianni thought for a bit. "Do we know someone who works for the telephone company? An installer or a lineman?"

They looked at him blankly.

"Someone who installs phones," Gianni repeated.

"I know one guy who lives on Mott Street, a couple of doors from my mother," said Gus.

"Good. Now we have to find a place to put in an extension line so we can get the call without having to be in the restaurant," said Gianni.

Frankie the Pig's eyes narrowed appreciatively. "How about the garage on Spring Street, right around the corner?"

"Do we know the people who own it?" asked Gianni.

"Sure," said Tony. "That's where Joey and I sell the swag clothes."

"Swag? We can't have anything to give the police an excuse to come in and arrest us," Gianni said.

"It isn't really swag," Tony explained. "The women love to buy clothes they think they're getting for a steal—you know what I mean? We used to have swag when we were kids. But for years now we've been going up to the garment center and buying this stuff—it's legit, but we can't tell our customers, because they wouldn't think they were getting such a steal."

Gianni laughed. "But for as long as this takes, we can't have women coming in and out of the place."

"That's easy," said Tony. "We'll tell them we're out of stock—our boys got caught highjacking a truck. They'll get a thrill out of that. It'll be even better for business."

"All right," said Gianni. "Now Gus, you know this telephone man?"

"A little, Gianni. Not real well."

"I want an extension line from Mike's phone booth installed in the garage. And have Mike put a sign inside his booth saying that it's out of order—I don't want anybody in a passing car to be able to see the sign."

"Okay, I'll get the guy first thing in the morning," said Gus.

"What do you mean, in the morning?" Frankie the Pig cut in. "Go and wake him up now. Tell him it's an emergency. It is, in case you don't know it."

"Okay, okay."

"Gus, tell him we need a favor and we'll appreciate it," said Gianni. "We'll owe him a favor in return. Tell him we want it in before morning, if possible," he added.

Gus left the restaurant.

"And we know nothing else about these people?" Gianni resumed.

"That's the problem," said Frankie the Pig.

Gianni put his elbows on the table and rested his chin in his hands, staring straight ahead. "They must know something about you. They know the make-up of the group, who's the boss and underboss. They didn't find that out reading comic books. They must be on the in."

"They might have gotten it from the newspapers, you know," said Philly the Splash. "Or from one of those bullshit charts they put together for the hearings."

"It's possible, I guess," said Gianni. "But it doesn't figure that somebody'd just read papers and get the idea to do something like this. After all, they're dealing with death, or so they'd figure."

"They sure are," said Bobby Matteawan.

"It'd have to be some tough guys," Gianni said. "Men with balls enough to come right into Mike's restaurant and get the number from the phone booth."

"Right," said Frankie the Pig. "Mike's regular number is listed, but not the booth number."

"Someone had to come straight into the lion's den to get it," Gianni continued. "No, they're not just people reading a newspaper."

"Maybe they're runners or something like that," said Tony, "working for somebody in the colored neighborhoods."

"That's a direct hit, Tony," said Gianni. "I was thinking somewhere in that area myself. How about Big Diamond Walker up in Harlem?" he asked Frankie the Pig.

"What about him?" Tony cut in. "He's one of my accounts."

"He may be able to give us something on this," said Gianni. "If not, he can get information faster than we could. Go up to Harlem and find him. Tell him what's what and see what he comes up with."

"But if colored guys are involved in this thing, why would Big Diamond help us?" asked Joey. "He could be in on it himself."

"He'll help because Big Diamond is an old-timer and rebels are enemies of all old-timers," said Gianni. "I doubt he'd be in on this. Everybody always treated him square, helped him make plenty in Harlem. Why would he want to upset the apple cart? And if he did want to take over, why grab Sal Angeletti? Sal's only the money man. He'd grab a numbers man first. No, this smells like some punks trying to make a score. Big Diamond doesn't need a score. But just in case, Tony, go over and look right into his eyes."

"I'll look, all right," said Tony. "He won't fool me."

"Take it easy, though, even if his eyes don't look good," said Gianni, "remember, somebody still has Sal. We have plenty of time to get them later." Gianni stared around the table. "Remember this: we want Sal back alive. Then we'll get whoever grabbed him and teach them a lesson."

Gianni reflected silently on his own words. It suddenly dawned on him that he didn't want to kill anyone, or have anyone killed. He realized he was speaking only to placate the others and urge them on. But what lesson would he condone? Violence was not his game any longer. *I've really gotten soft*, he thought. He pushed it aside. For the moment the only important thing was to find Sal.

Tony stood up.

"Take a couple of boys along," Gianni said.

"I don't need anybody just to go see a couple of niggers."

Gianni gave him a stern look. "Big Diamond is our friend. Remember that. Our business now is to get Sal back. And this is only round one: we're still feeling things out."

"Yeah, but remember how Tami Mauriello almost knocked Joe Louis on his ass when he came out fighting in the first round?" asked Bobby Matteawan.

"If we do that in this fight, the only prize we'll win is a dead Sal," Gianni replied.

"Remember that, Tony," said Frankie the Pig. "That's orders. Just go over and talk, and tell us what Big Diamond has to say, and what's in his eyes."

"Okay." Tony turned and walked out of the bar.

"There's another possibility besides the numbers," Gianni said. "Narcotics."

"What have we got to do with narcotics?" asked Frankie the Pig. "You know better than anyone that we don't fool around with that—we never did. And if any of our friends did and we found out, they know we'd be the first to kick them in the ass. It's that way all over town."

"All the big arrests are South Americans," said Gus. "Even the D.A. and the *Times* say the mobs aren't involved in that business."

"But there *are* a few tough guys who deal in it on the sly," said Gianni, "and they must have some pushers. Those pushers would have the knowledge and the balls to do this. We only have until eight o'clock tonight, and there's a lot of ground to cover. Let's start by going to see all the bosses in town—ask around, see what they've heard, just in case there's something in the wind."

"The big narcotics dealers?" asked Frankie the Pig.

"No," said Gianni, "I mean our friends. It's worth a shot. We don't have anything else to go on yet."

"I thought we wanted to keep this among ourselves," said Gus. "We don't want to let anyone else know—it's embarrassing."

"You can stop being embarrassed right now," said Gianni. "You did nothing wrong. It happens. The best people can be suckered out once in a while." Gianni looked momentarily at Frankie the Pig. "Anyway, if there's something in the wind, our friends may know of it. And if it's something new, they'll want to know about it to protect themselves."

"But it's late, Gianni," said Frankie the Pig. "We can't wake up bosses."

"Yes we can. This is important. Tell them I'm sending out word: I'm taking a special interest in this because it's Sal Angeletti. This time I'm putting myself on the line for Sal."

The others studied Gianni with new respect.

"Frankie, do you have any money?" asked Gianni.

Frankie fished into his pocket.

"Not pocket money. Ransom money. If they took Sal because they had a revenge or contract, we're not going to get him back at all. But if they took him for money, then we better start getting it together."

"You hear that?" Frankie the Pig asked the men around the table. "Start collecting money in the street, get it from people who owe us, people we take care of. All the money you can find. Tell them they'll get it back in a couple of weeks."

"Don't say anything about Sal," Gianni cautioned.

Gus picked up a newspaper from a nearby table and by habit turned to the horse page. "Look, here's a horse called Ransom running tomorrow, I mean tonight. Boy, that's a good shot."

"I'll give you a good shot," said Frankie the Pig. "Forget the horses, we've got work to do."

"Sal'd tell you it's worth a C note."

"Sal isn't going to the track or anyplace else unless we get him back."

"Don't worry, he'll be back," Gianni said. "He'll have to go to the track to win back all the ransom he's going to cost us."

3:00 A.M.

Yank parked his white Barracuda at the curb on St. Nicholas Avenue and turned off the engine. The windshield wipers stopped in midcourse and immediately the windswept rain blurred the glass. Even inside the car he felt the cold; he should have had the heater fixed. At least when Nita was with him, that soft package of quiet delight would snuggle against him. Shit, he thought, one day his woman would ride around in a big-ass Cadillac with a big-ass heater, grooving on the stereo. He smiled bitterly. Soon, soon there would be a real change.

Yank got out of the car, locked it, and made his way toward 123rd Street. The lot on the corner still contained the butcher's refrigerated counter from which watermelon, peanuts and vegetables were sold in summer. But now in the cold and wet it was padlocked. Someone had painted *Off the Pig* in red on the white porcelain.

Turning the corner Yank walked quickly toward a small building with a stoop. On one side of the stoop was a railing with a gate in the center, which led to the apartment of Sheila Cummins, the landlady. Usually Sheila was sitting in that basement window watching the street, but her lights were off now. Yank went up the stoop and opened the outer door. A bare bulb overhead revealed a set of four mailboxes in the left wall. None of them had name-plates; one had its door missing and two had holes where the locks should have been. Yank entered the inner door and was assailed by an acrid smell of urine. He stepped gingerly over a heap of plaster beside the first-floor apartment where some junkies had attempted to bore through the walls. The wooden wall studs and metal laths were exposed. Several sets of plaster-caked shoes had ascended the steps before him. He wondered if the others had all arrived.

Yank reached the top floor, then continued to the roof. He hesitated just inside the roof bulkhead for a few minutes, listening for footsteps behind him. It was totally silent except for the hum of a refrigerator out of phase somewhere. He pushed open the door and stepped onto the roof. In the darkness he put his foot into a puddle; immediately he felt the cold water soaking into his sock. Yank cursed as he moved deftly across the roof, over the parapet wall onto the adjoining roof, then ducked into the doorway leading down into the next building. Quickly he moved his tall, powerful frame down the stairs. Yank was about six-foot-three, well muscled from his basketball days in the playground and then Benjamin Franklin High School. His hair was moderately Afro, topping off his strong, handsome dark complexion.

Yank knocked on the door of apartment seven. He heard movement inside, then the peephole moved and the door opened.

"Where the fuck you been, man?" asked Hartley, the one who

opened the door. Hartley was short and thin, with a black pencil mustache. He was darker-skinned than Yank.

"Doing a little scouting," Yank said, moving into the apartment.

The other three were already there. Bull, who was just that—chunky, thick-necked, bald, very black. Alfred—light-skinned, sinister-looking, tall and thin—had a scar from the left corner of his mouth to his left cheekbone. The third was Duck, who like Yank was tall and powerfully built.

"What'd you see?" asked Bull.

"Nothing. I took a drive past the Two Steps Down Inn. Naturally, I didn't spend too much time—I just drove by. Nobody was there. The restaurant was closed and the lights were out. I didn't even see anybody on the street."

Bull raised his eyebrows, a little surprised. "I'd have figured them having a council of war, getting their guinea torpedoes all lined up."

Yank sat on the threadbare couch; Bull took a chair at the table in the middle of the room. Hartley went over to the sideboard, poured himself a drink from a bottle of Four Roses and cut it with Coke.

"Hey, Hartley, you really punishing that stuff," said Alfred.

"You mind?" said Hartley. "I don't mind you when you do your thing, sniffing your brains out."

"Can it!" yelled Bull, his eyes, which seemed small in his large head, blinking furiously.

"What do you figure, Bull?" asked Duck, his arms folded across his formidable chest as he leaned against the wall.

"What's to figure? They paid for the other three. These pigs'll pay too."

"Yeah, but the others were just trash compared to this guy, man—guys who controlled local numbers and books. This is the big leagues compared to them."

"They weren't that little, Duck. One guy handled all the bookies in upper Manhattan; another the same over in Boston Road and around there. And the other guy pushed half of all the junk in the south Bronx. We're going to shake whitey up so bad, he won't want the rackets in our territory—he's going to leave our turf to us. Besides, we got ourselves a hundred-fifteen thousand already, didn't we?"

"And killed a guy," said Hartley unhappily. "Don't you think, Bull, maybe we got enough already? I mean, a hundred-fifteen . . ."

"Can it! You want out?" Bull demanded, looking at Hartley with fierce eyes.

Hartley smiled placatingly. "No, Bull. You know I'm in, it's just that, well, why push our luck? We're doing all right now. I mean, a hundred-fifteen . . ."

"Man, you don't understand," said Bull. "It's not the money. It's getting out from under." He pounded his fist on the table. Hartley froze with apprehension. The others watched silently. Bull rose, his muscles rippling. "We been running errands, picking up numbers, booking bets, pushing junk for whitey too long! Black people's bread belongs to us blacks that can part them from it—not whitey!" Bull was snarling through clenched teeth. "We're going to run our own rackets and steal from our own people. The money we're making them cough up with the kidnaping and the guy we killed are only to show we have balls, man, balls, not watermelons between our legs— you got it?"

"Sure, Bull. I know all that," said Hartley.

"Well, remember it when you tell me we got enough. Nothing's enough until we have it all. All of it for ourselves. We're going to make whitey scared shitless to come into our neighborhoods."

"But how come this old man?" asked Duck. "He has nothing to do with Harlem or south Bronx. What are we grabbing him for?"

"Because he's a big man in the syndicate. All them wops and orga- nized crime are going to know we got them between our legs now. We grab him like we did, and all the small local guys'll shit green apples. We'll crack this town open in one shot, man—one shot!"

"Right on," said Yank. "Big Uncle Tom Diamond and everybody else'll fall right into line, 'cause we're going to pull this whole thing down from the top. They know we mean business now."

"Man, they must have shit when that body hit the street," said Alfred, smiling.

"And those guys uptown paying us twenty-six thousand," Bull roared. "Man, when we played them that recording and they heard that guy's voice, they paid us for a dead man." He walked over to the sideboard and poured a neat drink of whiskey. He sipped it, laughing, and slapped Alfred's palm in jubilation. "That was a cool idea."

"That's right, baby," said Alfred. He took out a small envelope and drew a pinch of cocaine, tapping back the excess before sniffing it deeply.

"They all small-timers compared to us now," said Bull. "We just hit our stride, man. We're in the league we belong in."

"Are we going to kill this old guy too?" asked Hartley.

"I haven't decided yet. If they don't pay, we'll cut his head off for them. If they pay, well, maybe we won't. Why stir up all these guinea torpedoes if we don't have to? We want to make money, not war."

"How much we going for, Bull?" asked Alfred.

"Plenty. This is the big league, isn't it? Say about a hundred thousand."

"You think they'll pay a hundred for that old man?" said Yank. "I wouldn't."

"They better," said Bull. He sat down again at the table. "They been squeezing money out of our shoe leather for a long time, baby, a long time."

"Man, let me cut him open and see what's inside a guy they'd pay a hundred thousand for," said Alfred with his sinister, crooked smile.

"Yeah, man, if we let this cat go back, he'll know what we look like and he'll have his boys come after us. Why leave witnesses?" asked Duck.

"Man, you know we all look alike to them pigs. Where they going to find us?"

"Me, I'm going to be gone with my bread," said Hartley..

"Oh, no you're not," said Bull. "We going to stay around here and take over when they start to thin out—that's the whole bit, man. We going to stay, doing our regular thing just like before, until it cools down a bit."

"What?" Alfred moaned. "After all this scheming and dreaming, we got to hold onto the bread and not spend it?"

"That's it," said Bull. "Unless you want someone to give you a real fine funeral with your share—which they'll do if they see some no-count nigger runner going around spending all kinds of bread."

"Oh, come on Bull, we got to spend some of it," said Yank. "Momma needs a nice warm heater attached to a nice new Coupe de Ville."

"Patience, baby. I want to sport with all the loot too. But in good time, baby. In good time we'll live like kings."

"What's good time?" asked Duck.

"Three, four months," said Bull.

"Shit, man," said Hartley, "that's like the Chinese water torture. Ain't we been doing without long enough?"

"And is three or four more months going to break your little ass?"

"Maybe, maybe it will, with all that bread sitting in your pocket doing nothing," said Hartley.

"Well, let me put it to you real straight, baby. What would you rather have break your ass: three or four months, or me?" Bull glared at Hartley menacingly. "'Cause you start sporting around town, and we all going to have our ass in a sling."

"Okay, okay, Bull," Hartley said.

"Alfred, you sure the old man is safe in Newark?" Bull asked.

Alfred nodded slowly, emphatically. "Sure is, man. He don't even know where he is. Duck had him blindfolded in the back of the car."

"And lying face down on the seat. He ain't got no idea where he is. And nobody else does either, except my cousin and Charlie, who're watching him."

"We going to give them a recording on this guy?" Hartley asked.

"Why, you soft on pigs today?" Yank smiled.

"Man, don't you pull that shit on me. I'm in this the same as you. I been dragging my ass pushing junk a lot longer than you, and my dues book is fuller than yours, so don't be talking trash to me. I just want to know we going to off this cat."

"Let's see what happens," said Bull, pouring another neat drink. "Let's just see what happens when we call them tonight."

"What'll you tell them?" asked Alfred.

"I'm going to tell them we want the hundred and no fucking around."

"When you going to tell them to have it?"

"By tomorrow night."

"You think they got that kind of bread hanging around?" Alfred asked, almost licking his lips.

"If they don't, they'll get it. That's their problem, baby. We got our own troubles."

9:45 A.M.

Gianni Aquilino looked at his wristwatch as Sandro Luca, his lawyer, opened the huge wooden door of the New York County Lawyers' building. Sandro was young, dark-haired and well-dressed. Gianni had known him since he was a boy; his uncle, before he had been deported to die in Italy, had been Gianni's friend and associate for many years.

"What time will this start, Sandro?" Gianni asked, thinking of the myriad things he had to do, details to sift and analyze, before eight this night.

"It's supposed to start at ten," Sandro replied, "but I don't know how many witnesses they'll call ahead of us."

The Chairman of the Joint Legislative Committee for the Investigation and Control of Crime, Maurice Stern of the New York State Senate, had chosen the County Lawyers' building not only because its auditorium and other facilities were more conducive to a crime probe than the State Office Building on Broadway, but also because it was a more dramatic and imposing setting for television and other news coverage. And, in the eyes of Senator Stern, news coverage was always a most important consideration, particularly in an election year.

Just inside the entrance was a sign marked HEARING with an arrow pointing up the marble staircase. Gianni and Sandro started climbing.

"Do you want a slip of paper with the Fifth Amendment typed out?" Sandro asked. "I brought one with me just in case."

Gianni smiled. "Sandro, *caro*, I could recite the Fifth Amendment in my sleep. I'm going to have it carved on my tombstone." He paused to light a cigarette.

They reached a center landing where the stairs split into two curving marble banks, rising to a large, somber anteroom. On one side, the anteroom opened onto the auditorium; on the other, into a large waiting room with a fireplace at each end where television cameras and lights were being set up.

Many small groups of men were huddled around the edges of the anteroom. As Gianni reached the top of the stairs, a wave of excitement quickly whipped through the reporters and cameramen. They surged toward him.

"Mr. Aquilino will testify inside, gentlemen," Sandro announced. "He won't make any statements other than that. I know you'll get pictures whether we want them or not—I only ask you to wait until we're leaving."

"As long as we get them then," said one of the cameramen.

"What's your name, counselor?"

Sandro told them, spelling it out.

The reporters were like ducks voraciously lunging for pieces of bread tossed in the water.

"Can we get a filmed interview, counselor?" asked one of the well-known ABC newscasters.

Gianni stood silently at Sandro's side, letting him handle it all.

"No. You'll get your pictures as we leave, but no interviews."

"How about inside when Gianni's testifying, counselor? Can we get a couple of shots in there?" asked another TV man. His cameraman stood next to him, camera in hand, focusing on Gianni.

Sandro and Gianni moved forward. "No pictures inside. You'll be able to take them on the way out."

"See if you can speed this up, Sandro," Gianni said in a low voice. "I've got to get out of here as soon as possible."

"Okay," Sandro said. "Will you be all right by yourself for a moment while I go inside?"

Gianni nodded with faint amusement.

"Hiya, Gianni," said one of the reporters, "how've you been?"

"Fine. How've you been?"

"Okay," replied the reporter. "Remember, I asked a lot of questions you didn't answer back when the Grand Jury was investigating that time you were shot?"

"Don't remind me," said Gianni.

The reporter smiled. "How about a statement?"

Gianni shook his head, smiled, and moved toward an empty chair against the far wall. He put down his hat and coat, took out his cigarette lighter, looking around the room as he did so. Although he knew many of the other witnesses waiting there, for all recordable purposes he did not recognize or react to anyone in the room. None of the witnesses reacted to him either. They were all aware that mixed in the crowd were local detectives, federal agents, prosecuting officials—some identifiable and others disguised as reporters and cameramen—who were watching their every move, recording their actions, noting who accorded more respect to whom, who knew whom, who spoke to whom, all later to be set down at length in official reports or family charts.

Sandro walked into the hearing room. On the speaker's stage several library tables had been assembled into one long table, with microphones strategically placed for the committee members. Sandro saw Senator Stern standing beside the stairs leading to the stage. He was of medium height, slim, with sharp features and red hair.

Stern smiled a thin crease of a smile. "Good morning, Sandro. You representing some of the people here?"

"Just one," said Sandro, "Gianni Aquilino."

Stern's eyebrows rose, his lips pursed as he nodded appre-ciatively. "Might as well represent a top man as long as you're here."

"What's that supposed to mean?" Sandro asked.

"Come on, Sandro. He's still one of the biggest men in the Giordano family—one of the biggest men in the Cosa Nostra until he stepped down. You know that as well as I do."

"All I know is what you tell me, Maurice."

A ruddy-faced, tall man walked up and joined them. Sandro recognized him as a state policeman attached to Stern's committee.

"Hello, counselor," he said distrustfully, studying Sandro as he might a suspected criminal. To him there was not much difference. Defense lawyers were trying to protect evil; therefore they too were evil.

Stern smiled. "Is your man going to testify this morning?"

"I don't believe he will," Sandro said.

"Do any of them ever?" asked the policeman.

"I thought the United States Constitution was still in force in New York State," said Sandro.

The trooper's face streaked with annoyance. "The Constitution's to protect honest citizens, not racketeers and hoodlums."

"Who's giving out the signs these days?" said Sandro.

The trooper stared at Sandro, trying to figure that one out.

"You know we have immunity powers now," said Stern. "If your man refuses to testify, the committee can grant him immunity. Then he'll have to testify because he's immune to prosecution; he can't claim the Fifth Amendment. If he refuses, he'll go to jail for contempt."

"I don't think your immunity is valid," Sandro said flatly.

"I wouldn't count on it," said Stern. "Why not?"

"Leave a few surprises in life, will you, Senator? What time do you think you'll get to my man?"

"In a few minutes. The reporters want to interview me before we start."

"That's very important."

"You think not? How else are the good citizens going to know what their committee is doing about crime?" Stern's face wore a thinly veiled smile. "You'll be third, I think. Just in time for the afternoon editions. After all, the Silver Eagle is good copy."

"All set, Mr. Chairman," announced a newsman, motioning Stern to accompany him to the waiting room. Sandro walked out behind them. He saw a cameraman standing poised to snap a picture of Gianni.

"Didn't I ask you to wait until later?" Sandro said, walking between them.

"Come on, counselor, I have to make the next edition—besides, I may not be able to get near you when you come out."

"Let him, Sandro. What's the difference," said Gianni. "They've got hundreds of pictures already. Only criminals have to hide. And this fellow's got to make a living."

"Thanks, Gianni," the photographer said, snapping a picture. Other photographers followed suit. Gianni sat impassively as strobe lights shattered the calm of the room. He could see Stern in the other room bathed in the television lights, speaking unheard words of self-praise and purpose.

"Got enough?" Gianni asked the photographers.

"Just a couple more. Hold it, please."

"Okay. If they're good, send me a couple," Gianni said, smiling.

The cameramen finished and walked off winding their cameras and writing picture credits on pads.

Gianni studied his watch. It was 10:30 already. "When will we be going in?"

"Shortly," said Sandro. "They have a couple of other witnesses before you. But you're one of the main attractions, it seems."

"I wish I could testify and answer their dumb questions," Gianni said. "The nonsense they ask is so old and out of date it's got hair on it. Besides they have all the answers already. But they don't really want answers; they want people to refuse to answer. That way the circus atmosphere is complete—the public gets scared and they get their appropriations."

"Why don't you testify, then?" asked Sandro.

"Because this way nobody gets hurt. It's always been done this way."

"I think the old rule of silence is wrong and out of date too," said Sandro. "When people go to prison for thirty days or even a year for refusal to answer, they do get hurt. And it's needless."

"How is it needless?" Gianni saw Joey reach the top of the stairs and stand at the edge of the room, searching the faces. "Wait a minute, Sandro."

Gianni signaled. Joey nodded and started across the room. His presence was duly noted by the investigators. Gianni knew this, but other considerations were more important right now.

"What is it?" Gianni asked. "Has the phone been moved?"

"It should be by now. And we locked up the dresses."

"Good. Any news from the boys we sent around town?"

"They're still out. Did you see the papers this morning?"

"No. What happened?"

Gianni took the copy of the *Daily News* Joey was carrying. He was aware of eyes watching his movements and he read the paper casually. The cover story was the antici-pated splashdown of Apollo 14. Gianni turned the page. Inside were pictures of the astronauts' children and wives, and stories of the war in Vietnam.

"What am I supposed to be looking for?" he asked softly, not looking up.

"Page 7. That's last night's body."

Gianni turned the pages slowly, reading every one in turn. Page 7 had a story about the finding of the body of a small-time hoodlum in the Hudson River, locked in the ice floes between the piers. Gianni read it with the same cursory attention he had given the other stories and moved on. The body was identified as a Tom Barton from the Bronx, several times arrested in connection with selling narcotics.

"Does anyone know him?" asked Gianni, not looking up, still turning the pages.

"No. But Gus said he thinks he's connected with some people from the south Bronx—just small-timers, guys who fool around supplying junk to pushers in the colored neighborhoods."

"Get someone up there right away. Find out about him. See if anyone knows why he was killed, or how."

"Okay. I'll go myself."

"And have everyone at the garage by six. We've got a lot of work to do." He handed the paper back to Joey with a courteous nod.

Senator Stern emerged from the waiting room and the press briefing that would reach all the television screens that evening. He walked into the hearing room and took his seat as Chairman of the Committee. Other members of the committee, state senators and assemblymen, sat on either side of him. Stern gaveled the room quiet, and called for the first witness. A squat, olive-skinned man in the anteroom put down his coat and entered the auditorium. The reporters and cameramen followed him in. The doors were closed behind them, leaving only other witnesses and a few detectives in the anteroom. Gianni's eyes met the eyes of another witness. The other man nodded. Gianni made no acknowledgement whatever.

"I imagine you'll be called soon," Sandro said. "Stern said you'd be third."

"I hope so," said Gianni.

Soon the photographers burst backwards from the auditorium, hovering about the door, setting themselves for something to emerge.

"Here he comes," one of the photographers called, and the strobe lights and flashbulbs began to flare. The witness shielded his face with his hand as he picked up his hat and coat, then started moving quickly through the phalanx of photographers toward the stairs.

"Go around the other stairs—go downstairs," called some of the photographers. They ran down the twin staircase to catch up with the witness as he reached the lower platform. The men with the more cumbersome motion picture cameras and the battery-operated lights had to be content with leaning over the railing to record the reluctant figure bounding down the stairs.

The doors to the auditorium were closed again, and a sign was placed in the oval window indicating EXECUTIVE SESSION. Gianni looked around. The other waiting witnesses were still standing in the anteroom. Sandro walked toward the doors.

A committee assistant standing guard shook his head as Sandro approached. "You can't go in, counselor. Sorry."

"Is there another witness on the stand?" Sandro asked.

The man at the door nodded, making sure to maintain his position so as to keep Sandro from entering.

As Sandro turned, he recognized Pete Scanlon, the building custodian, standing near an exit. Scanlon winked.

"How're you doing?" Sandro asked as he walked toward him.

"Okay, how's yourself?"

"Fine. Looks like they're having some fun here today."

"Yeah," the custodian replied, "but Stern's a little disappointed with the turnout. I heard some of the assistants talking."

"Not enough people coming to see what's going on?"

"The guys from the press. There're a lot missing," Scanlon said. "I guess they're at that hippie demonstration over at City Hall. It cuts into the coverage here."

"Were they expecting more?"

"Sure. They got piles of left-over information sheets in there, all with the names of the witnesses and their nicknames, the families they belong to, the whole thing." Scanlon fished in one of his shirt pockets and brought out a piece of paper. "Here's one of them," he muttered, handing over the still folded paper. Sandro put it in his inside jacket pocket. "They've got other info too, about the committee members. You want that?"

"No, I know the committee. Who've they got in there now?"

"It's their star for today," the custodian said, smiling. "Some guy with a black hood on—they got holes cut out for the eyes and he's supposed to know a lot about the mobs. He's supposed to give the inside story. It'll be today's big publicity."

"Is he on the information sheet?"

"Yeah, as Carmine Napoli—but his name is really Crawford, one of the cops told me. They brought him down from the penitentiary."

"I guess it makes it a little more exciting to give him an Italian name."

"Yeah, Stern really puts on a show," Scanlon chuckled.

Sandro walked back to Gianni. He sat next to him and unfolded the information sheet Scanlon had given him. "Here's the list of today's star performers," he said.

"Am I on it?"

"Yes. They have you down as Gianni Aquilino, also known as the Silver Eagle, also known as Johnny Quill."

"Who's Johnny Quill?" asked Gianni, frowning. "I'm not known as Johnny Quill—never was."

"That's what it says. It says you're now the *consigliere* of Vito Giordano's old family; the elder statesman."

"Great. They must have a fiction writer putting their scripts together. What else did they put down?"

"It says you've been arrested three times, with one conviction for unlawful possession of a weapon."

"That was 1928, maybe '30," Gianni said, "more than forty years ago. Imagine the crap they have to dig up to make a show here. I went to New Jersey carrying a pistol I was licensed to carry in New York, so I was arrested for it—I didn't have a New Jersey license. I showed them my New York license, pleaded guilty, paid ten bucks, and they took me to the ferry back to New York. That's the sum of horrible things I've done in my life to make me a gangster. This little squirt, Stern, really wants to make a name for himself. Every couple of years there's a new squirt looking for a name. There should be some way of preventing him from harassing people."

"He does have the right to subpoena you," Sandro replied; "but I agree, he can't just subpoena you for laughs. And that's how I think we can beat this immunity."

Flash units were going off inside the auditorium, the light flaring beneath the doors. "He can't prove there's a syndicate—but that's a long story," said Gianni. "I'll tell you some time. They must be almost finished in there. I'd like to get it over with."

"Gianni Aquilino," announced one of Stern's assistants at the door.

"Okay. We're on. Follow me," said Sandro. They walked in and faced the long committee table on the stage. Stern nodded and pointed to the witness table below. Gianni and Sandro sat down.

A photographer, raising his camera, walked crouching toward Gianni.

"Your Honor," Sandro addressed Stern with extra formality, "this witness does not wish to be photographed while he appears before the committee."

The photographer stopped, looking up toward Stern.

"Is your client ashamed to be photographed, Mr. Luca?" asked Stern.

"Whatever his reason, Your Honor, my client does not wish to be photographed. Although he wishes to cooperate with your committee as fully as he is able, he does not waive his personal rights just because some people are trying to garner publicity."

"Are you in some fashion disparaging the members of this committee?" Stern asked coldly.

"I hadn't intended to," Sandro answered. "I was referring to other witnesses. However, if any of the committee members happen to be publicity-hungry, unfortunately it refers to them too."

"All right, I'll not fence with you, Mr. Luca. No photographs will be taken while the witness is in this room. Let's get on with the questioning. Will you rise to be sworn, Mr. Aquilino."

Gianni rose. He raised his right hand, placed his left upon a Bible, and swore to tell the truth. He sat again.

"Before we begin, Your Honor," said Sandro, "as I read the applicable statutes regulating these proceedings, when testimony is taken at a closed session—that is, one not open to the public—there can be no dissemination to the public of any matters taking place during the proceedings, unless an order permitting such dissemination has been voted upon by a majority of the committee. This proceeding is a closed session—and yet I note the presence of many newsmen here. Such dissemination would be in violation of law, and even this committee would be guilty of a misdemeanor if it permitted dissemination of matters now transpiring before it, unless such an order exists. I must ask to see such order or ask you to remove all newsmen and other persons not members of the committee from this auditorium."

"This is not a closed session, Mr. Luca," replied Stern. "The newsmen may stay." The committee studied Sandro.

"It *is* a closed session, sir," Sandro said; "I note that the doors are closed, and your committee assistants are not allowing members of the public other than police or newsmen through that door. A sign on the door indicates, Executive Session—this *is* a closed session."

Stern studied Sandro, then the doors at the rear. "Well then, I'll open the doors and you can invite in anyone you wish. The closed doors were merely a precaution to protect the previous witness."

"Since the previous witness' identity is well known," said Sandro, "and only newsmen and policemen were permitted in here, the black mask seems to have been more melodrama than protection. Moreover, Senator, I'm not interested in inviting anyone to this proceeding. I merely wish to have the letter of the law obeyed, as, I am sure, do you. I wouldn't want any member of this honorable commission to be guilty of a misdemeanor."

Stern's face creased. "I might retain you—you'd have another client."

"I'd be delighted, sir."

"Open the doors and let's proceed," Stern instructed. The assistants opened the doors. Scanlon was grinning.

"Mr. Aquilino," Stern said, "before we proceed, two exhibits are being placed on your table. One is the picture of a person; that is Exhibit One. The other, of a house, is Exhibit Two. Now, what is your name?"

"Gianni Aquilino."

"Where do you reside?"

"Chickapea Road, Pawling, New York."

"Will you please look at Exhibit One. Who is that pictured there?"

Gianni was looking at a picture of himself as a younger man. "I respectfully decline to answer on the ground of my absolute constitutional right to do so."

"Is it not a picture of yourself, Mr. Aquilino?"

"I respectfully decline to answer on the ground of my absolute constitutional right to do so."

"You're not ashamed of your own picture, are you, Mr. Aquilino?"

"I respectfully decline to answer on the ground of my absolute constitutional right to do so."

"Would you look at Exhibit Number Two, sir."

Gianni was looking at a picture of a sunlit house, surrounded by huge shade trees. He leaned over to Sandro. "This isn't my house—it's a house about a mile from mine."

"You don't have to repeat the same thing over and over," Sandro said, "just say, 'same answer.'"

"Is that your home, Mr. Aquilino?"

"Same answer."

Stern's eyes narrowed slightly. "Are you also ashamed of your own house?"

"Same answer," replied Gianni calmly. He leaned over to Sandro again. "You know, it takes a little twit like that to try to belittle people. I'd really like to take the bastard on."

"Don't get angry," Sandro said softly. "That's exactly what he wants you to do."

"Hell will freeze first," said Gianni. He sat back, calmly awaiting the next question.

"Are you a member of what is known as the Cosa Nostra?"

"Same answer."

"Are you a member of the family of Sal Angeletti, formerly the family of Vito Giordano, formerly your own family, you now being the *consigliere* of that family?"

The newsmen were copying every question, just as Stern wanted them to.

"Same answer."

"What answer is that, Mr. Aquilino?"

"Same answer," Gianni said coolly.

"I asked you to which answer you were referring, Mr. Aquilino?"

"Same answer."

Stern's complexion flushed slightly with anger. Gianni saw it and felt somewhat pleased to be having some fun too.

"Are you also known, sir, as the Silver Eagle?"

"Same answer."

"And you have also been known as Johnny Quill?"

"Same answer."

"And in a book by Joseph A. Lockwood, known as *Valachi Speaks*, on page 276 it says that Gianni Aquilino, also known as the Silver Eagle, has been arrested three times, was convicted only once of illegal possession of a weapon, is now the *consigliere* of Sal Angeletti's family, and in semiretirement from the Cosa Nostra. In 1959, an attempted execution of Aquilino took place in the lobby of his plush apartment building, after which Aquilino stepped down as the head of the family now headed by Sal Angeletti. Although retired, he is still an important and very active force in the Cosa Nostra. Is that true?"

Before Gianni had a chance to say anything, Sandro reached for the microphone. "Are you asking, Sir, whether it is true that Joseph A. Lockwood wrote the book, or whether it is true that the book is called *Valachi Speaks*, or whether it is true that such statement appears on page 276?"

"I want to know if the facts stated therein are correct," Stern said impatiently.

"Same answer," said Gianni.

"Are you retired from the Cosa Nostra, Mr. Aquilino?"

"I object to the question," Sandro cut in, "since you have not first established that the witness has ever been a member of such an organization—or even that such an organization exists."

"Assuming, Mr. Aquilino," said one of the other members of the committee, seated to Stern's left, "that you had been a member of this organization, are you now retired?"

"The assumption is improper and totally meaningless, Your Honor," said Sandro.

"The witness may answer it."

"Same answer."

"Mr. Aquilino, if we continue to ask you questions, are you going to continue to give the same answer?" Stern realized with a slight wince that he had repeated Gianni's own words.

"Same answer."

"You will not answer any questions?"

"Same answer."

"We'll adjourn this witness at this time, until the committee decides whether or not it wishes to grant Mr. Aquilino immunity. If immunity is granted, Mr. Aquilino, you know of course that you will be bound to testify or face being held in contempt, with a possible jail sentence?"

"Same answer."

"Mr. Luca, will you kindly advise your client of the implications of our granting immunity."

"Yes sir, I shall."

"Adjourned until February 11," said Stern. "Return then."

"That's two days from now. I need more time," Gianni said to Sandro.

"Your Honor," said Sandro, "I will need some additional time—"

"Thursday the eleventh," Stern was pleased to command. "No delays."

"Very well, sir," said Sandro.

Gianni and Sandro made their way toward the rear doors, the reporters backing from the room before them. Gianni walked out calmly, putting on his overcoat.

"You don't have to be in the pictures if you don't want to, Sandro," said Gianni. "It may be bad publicity for you."

"I haven't done anything wrong either," said Sandro.

Gianni smiled at him. They walked down the stairs amidst the flashing lights. Reporters thrust microphones in Gianni's face; movie cameras were whirring; voices and bodies surrounded them. Gianni kept smiling, moving silently through the crowd. They reached the cold air outside. It was still raining.

1:00 P.M.

Tony sat in the passenger seat as the car crossed Park Avenue at 125th Street in Harlem. Louie the Animal was driving. The cold rain was still fierce as they passed the big discount stores, the furniture stores, the pawnshops, the spare-rib counters, the bars, all with their windows battened.

"Well, at least they've got good weather for the splashdown," said Tony.

"What the hell splashdown?" said Louie the Animal. "Hey, you stupid nigger!" he shouted as a woman dodged in front of them to catch a bus.

"The men on the moon," said Tony. "Don't you read the papers?"

"Oh, yeah, yeah. I forgot," said Louie. "Do you think it had anything to do with the earthquake in California this morning?"

Tony glanced impatiently at him. "Of course not. They've been sliding into the ocean for years—people are crazy to live out there."

"You know they've already pinched looters cleaning out houses of people who left because of the flood," said Louie the Animal. He turned the car onto Lenox Avenue, heading uptown.

"Probably niggers," Tony said, studying the street ahead. "Who else'd make a score on people running for their lives?"

Louie pulled up to the curb near 134th Street.

Tony opened his door. "Come on," he said.

Louie the Animal looked at him. "Do I bring something with me?"

"Yes."

Louie the Animal slid the .38 revolver from beneath the dashboard and stuck it under his belt. They got out of the car and started across the sidewalk.

"In all the time I've been coming here, this is the first time I've been inside with you," said Louie the Animal.

Tony studied the street. Overhead was a huge neon sign, unlit now in midday: THE KINGS INN—DINING-COCKTAIL-LOUNGE. Louie the Animal opened the front door; Tony followed him in.

Inside it was almost as dark as night. The bar was long, sheathed in shiny red tufted vinyl, with mirrors behind the bottles. Toward the back was a dance floor, and many tables covered with red cloths.

The bartender was wiping the bar before setting a drink in front of an early customer. He looked up, hesitating just long enough to show apprehension; he saw the deadly earnestness on Tony's face. He glanced at Louie the Animal. The man the bartender was serving was very dark, almost the African blue-black, with bright piercing eyes. He examined the two white men. At the far end of the bar two other men were talking. They too stopped, studying the white men peering into the back. They resumed a subdued conversation, but were continually aware of the newcomers.

Tony ignored them, pulling Louie's sleeve and walking toward the back. He had learned early in life that in the street you never show fear or hesitation. Those emotions had smells all their own, and if someone caught scent of them you were already on the way down for the count.

The very dark man with the piercing eyes got off his stool and followed them slowly. Tony, who was casing the room as he walked, caught sight of him in the mirror along the bar. He watched the mirrored image's hands and kept walking. Big Diamond Walker was seated at his usual table with another man. The other tables were empty. He was large, rotund and dark-skinned, his graying hair neatly combed. He wore a well-fitting suit, and in the center of his tie a gold stickpin held a good-sized diamond. On the pinky of his right hand was a ring with an even bigger diamond. The man with him was medium dark and had a thin mustache. He wore a dark suit, dark gray shirt and white tie.

"Hello, Big," said Tony.

"Hey, Tony," said Big Diamond with a wide smile. "What are you doing here? Don't tell me I shortchanged you?" He too recognized the look on Tony's face but was playing it light.

"I've got some trouble I'd like to see you about," said Tony.

Big Diamond looked at Louie the Animal, then again at Tony. "Say hello to Lloyd, Tony. I don't think you've ever met."

Tony stepped forward and shook Lloyd's hand. It was powerful and he let you know it.

"This is Louie," said Tony. Louie nodded.

"Come on—sit down, sit down," said Big Diamond. He lit a long, fat cigar, turning to the dark-skinned man who had followed them from the bar. "Junior, go up front and tell Saul to bring us a bottle of Chivas." As Junior hesitated, he said, "Go ahead, Junior, these people are our friends."

"Wait outside, Louie," said Tony.

Louie nodded and made his way toward the door.

Saul the bartender brought the bottle of Chivas and set down glasses with ice in them. He poured a drink into the half-full glass in front of Big Diamond and set the open bottle in the center of the table. "Come on, Saul, take care of Tony—I said friend, didn't I?"

Saul poured Tony a drink and freshened Lloyd's.

"And buy a drink for Louie at the bar," said Big Diamond. "Good times," he said to Tony, raising his glass.

Tony just nodded as he sipped his drink.

Big Diamond put down his glass and puffed his cigar. "I'm sure this isn't a social call, Tony. What's up? How can I help?"

Tony studied Lloyd, then looked to Big Diamond.

"Lloyd's my main man, Tony. He's my main man," said Big Diamond, putting his arm on Lloyd's shoulder. "You talk to me, you talk to Lloyd, it's just the same."

"We got ourselves a problem downtown last night," Tony said slowly; "some guys, colored guys—punks!" he said purposely. He wasn't afraid and he wanted them to know it. Lloyd watched him carefully. "They grabbed my boss—snatched him. They've got him somewhere."

Big Diamond was shocked. "They grabbed Sal? I can't believe it."

"Believe it."

"What makes you think they were colored?" asked Lloyd. He had a deep, bass voice.

"I don't think," said Tony. "I know. They drove down the street and threw a dead man on our doorstep. Then they called us. I spoke to the guy myself. He was a—" Tony hesitated.

"Let's not have any of this colored, black, nigger bullshit," Big Diamond cut in. "We're talking serious business now. Any punk comes along and snatches one of the bosses—your bosses, my bosses—is a shiftless, rebel nigger." Big Diamond poured a drink all around. "Then what?"

"They said they'd call back at eight tonight. Now Gianni's sent us out all over town to get whatever information we can."

"Johnny who?" asked Lloyd.

"Gianni Aquilino."

Lloyd's eyes opened wide at the name.

Big Diamond smiled. "I knew the Old Silver Eagle'd come swooping off his perch again one day. What a man he is," he said to Lloyd. "What times we've had together. I mean real times. We used to meet at the clubs downtown. That man sure knows how to live. So Gianni sent you here?"

"Yes, to see if we can find anything—you'd have a better nose for this sort of thing than we would downtown, if you see what I mean."

Big Diamond nodded, puffing his cigar. "What do you know about it, Lloyd? You hear anything around?"

Lloyd shook his head.

"Don't just shake your head, Lloyd," said Big Diamond. "These are our friends and if we can help them, we're going to help them. We're all in the same game. If some white guys snatched me, you bet your ass you'd go down and ask them to help us. And they'd help us. We've been working together hand in hand for years. We get our money down there. If some punks come along and try cutting into them, they're cutting into all of us."

Lloyd looked skeptical.

"Come on, Lloyd," said Big Diamond. "They'll snatch the white bosses first, sure. Then you know who's next on the list?" He watched Lloyd, puffing his cigar. His pinky ring glistened momentarily.

"You got it baby. Me. Or Elmo. Or Stan. Now—you know anything about it, Lloyd?"

"I haven't heard a thing. I doubt it's our people, though." He looked at Tony. "The cats with us, I mean."

"Maybe not. But you can get better information on colored guys than we can," said Tony.

"That's for sure," said Big Diamond. "What do you think, Lloyd?"

"Maybe some of the militants—the Panthers," said Lloyd.

"Muslims?" Tony suggested.

Big Diamond shook his head. "No, they're not into that, it's not their way. They're more religious; they don't want to snatch one guy. And if it's the militants, they've got to be tough guys too," said Big Diamond. "I mean, you're not going to find any civil rights guys with the balls to get involved in this. They've got to be closer to us than just across the street."

"That's what Gianni thought," said Tony.

"Gianni's right. I'm right too," Big Diamond laughed. He offered the bottle around. The other two shook their heads. "Now, the question is: who? Start thinking close to us, Lloyd, close to the other mobs. If we don't come up with anything, then we'll spread the circle."

"It just can't be any of our people," said Lloyd. "Things are going too smooth, everyone's making plenty. I'd know, anyway."

"It's not the close men you've got to worry about," said Tony, "but the guys who hang around with them—their runners or pushers or whatever the hell they are."

"That's where it is," agreed Big Diamond. "The little guys that see the action but don't get as much of it as they want—they're always hungry."

"I'll talk around," said Lloyd.

"There isn't much time," Tony reminded.

"Right," said Big Diamond. "People who can do this can kill. They already have. Lloyd, get out there and do some talking right away. It shouldn't be long before you come up with a lead, if it's from up here. You've got to think of Brooklyn and the Bronx too, Tony."

"We know. There's a lot of ground and not too much time."

"I'll go see Elmo and Stan," said Lloyd.

"That's it, Lloyd. But take only Junior with you. If it gets around that we're looking, they'll go underground. Right now they must think they're safe because the white mobs can't get to them up here."

"Good thinking," said Tony.

"Yeah, once in a while we lift our heads out of the watermelon long enough to think a little," said Lloyd.

Tony stared at him.

"Hush that trash, Lloyd. These guys are just like us and we're like them. We're just different colors, that's all. The one color we all agree on is green—long, Uncle Sam green."

Tony nodded with as close to appreciation as was in him.

"Let me talk to you a minute," said Big Diamond. He rose. He just kept rising. Big Diamond was more than six-foot-four; he towered over five-foot-five Tony as he walked off to the side with him.

"Tell that Silver Eagle I said hello. And," Big Diamond spoke more softly now, "if he needs some bread for the ransom, tell him just to send the word to Big Diamond." He clapped Tony on the back.

"I sure will," said Tony, putting out his hand. His thin mouth defrosted slightly, only for an instant.

3:00 P.M.

Detective First Grade John Feigin turned from Mulberry Street and walked up the steps of P.S. 21, crossing the courtyard to the main entrance. It was one of the old style New York public schools, built like a limestone castle with turrets and gabled roof. How many thousands of kids had gone to this school, he wondered—how many thousands of hoods and punks, as well as decent people who now owned the stores on Mulberry and Mott Streets and the old buildings in Little Italy.

Feigin entered and started up the stairway. A couple of straggling kids were walking through the halls. He had just wasted an entire day in court on a collar he had made—some young punk breaking into a store and assaulting the owner, who lived in the back. All day in that lousy court, and the judge gave the lawyer a postponement on some flimsy excuse just barely veiling the fact that the lawyer hadn't yet received his fee.

Feigin was disgruntled, and a little out of wind, when he reached the third floor. He went right to the locked room where the tape recorder was set up. The tape was voice-activated, so it only recorded when someone was actually talking in the telephone booth at the Two

Steps Down Inn. Feigin opened the door and saw that an inch of new tape had wound through the sound heads.

Well, maybe we got something this time, he thought as he rewound the used spool and replaced it with a fresh one. They'd had the booth wired hoping to get a lead on a recent homicide. Feigin put the used tape in a small Manila envelope in his pocket. He reset the machine to Record, locked the room and made his way downstairs and back to the station house.

"Did you get anything?" asked Quinn, Feigin's partner. He was sitting at his desk in the squad room, two-finger typing a report.

"Yeah—a sore ass sitting in court all day till the lawyer showed. Then he got an adjournment." Feigin took various papers and the tape out of his pockets. "Papers and pigeons are going to take over the goddamn world," he muttered. "I don't know, twenty years on this job ought to be enough for anybody, but not me," he said, moving around to his desk. "Me, I've got perseverance—twenty-three years here already."

"I know, I know," said Lieutenant Schmidt, coming out of his office in shirtsleeves. "You're ready to toss in your papers, right?"

"Okay, Lou, rub it in. Just because I'd have nothing to do except drive my wife around, which is even worse than this lousy job." Lou was police argot for lieutenant.

Schmidt laughed and walked to the file cabinets against the far wall. The squad room was painted the familiar light green with white ceiling, a color scheme chosen about fifty years earlier because it was supposed to be easy on the eyes. From the looks of it now, the paint job must have been done then too, and not touched since. The room contained six desks, old wooden jobs, each with a typewriter and a phone. In one corner was a detention cage, and in another was a wall shelf where prisoners were fingerprinted. On the other side two partitioned cubicles served as lieutenant's office and clerical office. Between them was a door with a two-way mirror used when witnesses had to view suspects.

"What have you got?" Schmidt said to Feigin.

"A new tape from the wire at the Two Steps Down Inn, on the homicide over in Crosby Alley."

"That body we found shot in the back of the head?"

"That's the one," said Quinn, resting his two typing fingers. He lit a cigarette, blowing out a long stream of smoke that rose to the globe hanging from a chain in the center of the room.

"What's on the tape?"

"I haven't listened to it yet. Probably just some more of that garbled talk they use so we don't know what the hell they're saying—'I went to see that fellow, you know who I mean'" Quinn mimicked.

Schmidt laughed. "If there's anything on it, let me know."

Feigin went into the clerical office. On the desk was an old tape machine. Quinn came in as he was threading the tape into it.

"You want a cup of coffee, Jack?" Quinn asked as he ran water into the pot.

"No, thanks, Quinny. I had plenty of that poison they make in the luncheonette over in court."

Quinn set the pot on the hot plate and leaned his rump against the desk as Feigin started the tape rolling. Just as predicted, it recorded the conversations of various people who frequented the restaurant, all talking in vague terms intended to foil just such a tape. There was an occasional call from a patron to his home or a girlfriend, and from a couple of neighborhood people speaking in Italian to Con Edison or the telephone company.

"Wait a minute—what the hell is that?" said Quinn, holding up his hand.

They listened. They heard the voice of the man with the Southern accent talking to Tony, telling him they had Sal, and about a body that had been dumped.

Feigin stopped the machine abruptly and replayed the tape.

"It sounds like Mike speaking first, then Tony Mastropieri," said Feigin.

"Yeah—talking to a jig."

They listened intently, watching the spools wind.

"Get the Lou," said Feigin.

They played it for Schmidt. His eyebrows raised. He motioned to hear it again. "That sounds like a snatch—as though someone's got Angeletti," he said.

"And dumped a body," said Quinn.

"When was this tape made?" Schmidt asked.

"Had to be last night or early this morning," said Feigin. "I changed the spool yesterday afternoon."

"Anybody find a body near there?"

"Fat chance," said Quinn.

Schmidt nodded. "They'll get another phone call tonight."

"That's right. Tonight at eight," said Feigin. They all looked at their watches.

"A kidnaping right here in our own safe little neighborhood," said Quinn. "That's unusual. I mean, I thought that sort of thing, with ransom calls and all, went out with the old Mustache Petes."

"That wasn't a Mustache Pete they were talking to," said the lieutenant. "It sounded like a colored man."

"You figure they'll call back asking for ransom?" asked Feigin.

"If they just wanted to kill Angeletti, they wouldn't bother to call," Schmidt replied. "They'd have dumped him by now."

"But a colored guy!" said Quinn—"there aren't any connected with people down here."

"There aren't any colored guys down here, period," said Feigin. "Anyway, who the hell would want to snatch Angeletti? Who'd be crazy enough to tangle with that mob?"

"Somebody who knows something," said the lieutenant.

"How do you mean?"

"They knew enough to snatch Sal. They know Frankie the Pig is second in command. They had to get that information from somewhere."

"Some colored guys in the rackets maybe," said Feigin. "They'd know the setup."

"I can just see that wop Frankie the Pig going crazy," Schmidt bellowed. "He's probably wrecked half the neighborhood by now. Remember how we needed five guys to hold him down last time we collared him?"

They laughed.

"He's a tough bastard," said Feigin.

"There's one other group that would know the setup," said the lieutenant; "it's far-fetched, but we don't have much to go on right now."

"Who's that?" asked Quinn.

"Cops—Feds, or somebody like that."

"Why would it be cops?"

"It doesn't have to be; it's just that they'd know the setup too."

Feigin shrugged. "What for?"

"For money, what else?" chimed Quinn.

"It's not a bad idea, now that you mention it," said Feigin. "I could retire with a nice little nest egg—why didn't I think of that?"

Lieutenant Schmidt grinned at him. "I think you two ought to be over at the listening post tonight to cover that eight o'clock call. Take an extra set of headphones—we've got some around here somewhere."

"I was supposed to take my wife shopping tonight," said Feigin.

"Well now you've got an assignment, so give her a call."

"Yeah, yeah, and listen to her bitching for half an hour."

"You see, that's why you don't toss your papers," said Quinn.

3:30 P.M.

Bobby Matteawan stood on the sidewalk in front of 6930 Fourth Avenue in Brooklyn, studying the windows on the second floor. Gold lettering indicated JOHN MARASCO, REAL ESTATE, INSURANCE. Matteawan entered the building and climbed the stairs. Once inside the office, he took off his fedora, which he always wore with the brim up all around, and waited for the secretary to finish a phone call. She wasn't a bad piece, he thought as he watched her. She didn't have a tit in the world, but she was cute. He knew Frankie the Pig wouldn't have looked at her; he liked them with big bombs.

"Can I help you?" she asked, turning to him without a smile. Her face was hard, even under the heavy eyelashes and make-up. Her hair was the metallic black that comes with dyeing.

"I want to see Mr. Compagna."

"Mr. Compagna isn't here right now. Who can I say was here to see him?" she asked, poising her pencil over a pad.

"Gianni Aquilino sent me to see him," Bobby Matteawan said flatly.

The girl studied him for a moment. "Maybe Mr. Marasco can help you." She picked up the phone and pressed a button. "Someone here wants to see Mr. Compagna. He says he was sent by a Mr. Aquilino."

Marasco, a short, heavyset man with a mustache, appeared in the door behind her.

"Can I help you?"

"I wanted to see Mr. Compagna," Bobby Matteawan repeated.

"He's not here right now," Marasco replied. Another man, young and powerfully built, who had been inside with Marasco, also came to the door. A hand of cards was still furled in his right fist.

"You know when he'll be back?" Bobby Matteawan asked. "It's important. Gianni Aquilino sent me."

The man with Marasco put down his cards on the girl's desk and went out the front door. Bobby Matteawan heard him going downstairs.

"If you'll have a seat," said Marasco, "I'll see if I can get in touch with him." He went back into his office.

Bobby Matteawan sat on a chair and picked up an issue of *Life*. He leafed through it even though he had read it six months before. The girl took out a compact, primping her hair with one hand as she looked in the mirror. She moved her head this way and that to view the entire black mound atop her head. Bobby Matteawan thought it all looked like a cake up there.

Footsteps sounded on the stair. Bobby Matteawan watched the door. The man who had been with Marasco entered, followed by Compagna. The boss of one of the Brooklyn mobs, Compagna was tall and slender, with graying hair. Then came another man, a bit younger, heavyset, with black eyes.

"You wanted to see me?" Compagna said to Bobby Matteawan.

Bobby Matteawan looked at the two now standing behind Compagna. He stood up. "Yes. Gianni Aquilino sent me to talk to you: it's important."

"Come inside," said Compagna, walking into the office. The other two followed him. Marasco nodded and wordlessly left the room as Compagna sat behind the desk. On the wall over his head was a real estate broker's license with the name Philip Compagna typed in. "Now, what's your name?"

"Bobby Matteawan."

"Okay. Where is Gianni Eagle now?"

"Right now?"

Compagna nodded.

"He went to a crime hearing this morning, but he should be back at the—" Bobby Matteawan was about to say garage, "—at the place by now."

"What place?"

"Two Steps Down Inn."

"Angeletti's hangout." Compagna nodded to the young, powerful man who was leaning against the wall. He left the room. The other man sat in a chair next to the desk, facing Bobby Matteawan.

"How is Gianni? I haven't seen him in years," said Compagna, "even though we're both in real estate. He handles big deals in New York and all around the country. I'm just a small broker in this area. How is the Eagle?"

"He's fine," said Bobby Matteawan.

Compagna and the other man remained silent, waiting for something.

Shortly the powerful young man returned. He nodded. "Aquilino isn't there, but this man's okay with them."

"Good meeting you, Bobby," Compagna said, leaning over the desk. Bobby Matteawan stood up to shake his hand. "Shut the door, Sonny," Compagna instructed. The young man did so, remaining inside. "This is Nat, my *comparda*," Compagna said, introducing the man in the chair. "And this is Sonny."

Bobby Matteawan shook hands with them. Then he recited the events of the evening before, of the body dumped at the Two Steps Down Inn, and of the meeting with Gianni and his instructions. He inquired if Compagna had heard anything or knew anything which might help in tracking down the kidnapers.

"*Minca*," said Nat. "They even dumped a body—they're not fooling around."

"Since when do coloreds go around snatching us?" Compagna jutted his chin forward. "*Atzo!* They must be nuts. Who was the stiff they dumped? One of your people?"

"No. We didn't know who he was till we saw his name in the papers this morning. We dumped him in the river and the cops found him there," said Bobby Matteawan.

"Imagine it, snatching one of our friends; I can't believe it," said Compagna, shaking his head. "What kind of world is this getting to be?" He looked around at them.

"What kind of respect can you expect from a *tutzone*?" Nat asked.

"I expect to chop their fucking nigger heads off," Bobby Matteawan said, "but first we've got to find them. That's why I'm here. Gianni wanted to check with all the mobs to see if anyone knew anything."

Compagna shook his head. "You know anything about it, Nat?"

"Nothing except what I read in the papers. But if the guy they fished out of the river was the one dumped on your doorstep, I know who he's connected with."

"He's the same," said Bobby Matteawan anxiously.

"His name is Mike Wallace. I remember him from the time we had that business with Jerry the Jew in Manhattan."

"Oh yeah, all the way up on the other side of Harlem," said Compagna. "He was with Jerry?"

"He controlled one of his banks," Nat said. "I remembered him when I read about it. That's all I can tell you."

Compagna shrugged. "In this section—Bay Ridge and Benson-hurst—we don't have much to do with coloreds, you know? You go see Jerry," he said to Bobby Matteawan; "I'm sure Gianni knows him. Otherwise you can use my name. Meanwhile, I'll send Sonny around to see all the people we're friendly with, and I'll find out if anybody's heard anything more."

"That's good," said Bobby Matteawan, rising.

Compagna extended his hand, looking in Bobby Matteawan's eyes. "And say hello to Gianni Eagle. Tell him I send him my best regards."

"I will."

"Don't forget—my best regards."

"I won't forget."

Sonny opened the office and nodded to Bobby Matteawan as he

made his way toward the stairs. Bobby Matteawan put his hat on as he walked past the secretary, looking at her again as he left. Again she was twisting her head this way and that, looking in the little mirror at the cake on her head.

Gus was driving along Arthur Avenue in the Bronx. Next to him was a young man whom Mario Siciliano, boss of the Fordham Road section, had sent along to introduce him to a wise guy over on Webster Avenue. Wise guy, in street talk, means someone who engages in illegal activities. This wise guy on Webster Avenue, Charlie Guglielmo, was not connected with Mario Siciliano's mob or any of the others. He was an independent, an outsider, ostracized because he dealt in narcotics, mostly in the colored sections. None of the connected wise guys openly dealt with drugs; if they ever did, they had to be extra careful—fearful in the first place of the authorities, and more so in the second place lest the mob bosses discover it. In that event, punishment could be less just and more rapid.

Mario Siciliano told Gus that he had heard through the grapevine that this Guglielmo, called Gugi, had been the victim of a kidnaping extortion involving his grandson and some colored people.

The young man instructed Gus to turn a corner. He was dark-haired and handsome, wearing a leather jacket and a blue knit shirt and his hair was styled. Gus thought that if some of the older bosses saw him they'd think he was more a *riccune* than a wise guy.

"This is the place."

The place was a sleazy bar named The Horse's Tail. Inside, the bartender was adjusting the levers on the beer draughts.

"*Minca*," said Gus, "he really ought to fix them—this joint smells like they poured the beer all over the floor."

The bartender, sleeves rolled to the forearms, white apron tied in front of his barreled torso, looked up.

"Gugi around?" asked the young man.

The bartender wordlessly jerked his head toward the back.

Gus and the young man walked on. In the first booth was a man about fifty years old. He was not stocky but he had a full jowled face, and when he looked up, one of his eyes was at a weird angle. He needed a shave.

"Gugi?" asked the young man.

The man nodded. With napkin tucked under his chin, he had been bent over a plate of spaghetti and meatballs. He looked up at his visitors as, with fork and spoon, he finished pushing more than a mouthful of spaghetti into his maw. He sucked up the straggling strands, nipping the rest with his teeth.

"That's right," he said. He reached for a piece of bread and dipped it into the sauce.

"Mario sent me to see you," said the young man with regal authority.

Gugi put down the bread and studied the young man warily. He glanced at Gus, then back to the young man, his bad eye rolling sharply.

"What's the matter?"

"No trouble. We want some information."

Gugi seemed relieved. He leaned back and took a toothpick out of a shot glass on the table. "You guys want a drink or something?"

"No thanks. This is Gus. He's a good friend of ours," said the young man.

"Hello, Gus," Gugi nodded. "Sit down."

"Listen Gugi, I've got a lot of things to do and I don't have much time," said Gus. "One of our guys was snatched by some niggers. I understand you had the same kind of trouble recently. Is that right?"

Suddenly, Gugi's bad eye started to go wild. He rose in the booth with a full head of fury. "Those *putigida madonna sfarcime* niggers," he bellowed, standing now in the aisle. "Sure I had trouble—*bitze fidend, cournoud e merda.*" Gugi's clenched fist crashed on the table. The plates jumped. "Those miserable coward bastards come into my house to snatch me, you know? I was there with my grandson Charles, and that *disgratziada*, scum of the earth, that black *mulanyom merda* comes in with a gun—right in my house—and then instead of snatching me, he says he's going to kill my grandson!" The mere repetition of the fact made him shake with fury. "Those miserable black cocksuckers," he raged. "My grandson!—the poor little kid was scared to death. I'll kill those black, miserable spineless bastards with my bare hands. I'll cut them into little pieces!" Gugi grabbed a knife and plunged it into the tabletop, where it quivered in the formica.

The bartender looked back momentarily and continued with his work.

"That's really scum, ain't it?" the young man said to Gus. "I mean, it takes scum to threaten a kid."

"Scum of the earth," said Gus, now more concerned than ever. People who would threaten a kid wouldn't care what they did to Sal. "You know them?" he asked Gugi.

"If I knew them, they'd be dead already—dead, cut in pieces. *Putigida*," he fumed, turning in a circle, his clenched fists raised to the ceiling.

"Did they hurt the kid?" asked Gus.

Gugi shook his head. "I gave them fifty big ones. What else could I do?"

"I understand you do business with *yoms*," said Gus. "Maybe they work for you or know someone who does?"

"Believe me I've figured all those angles," Gugi said.

"I put all the guys who hustle for me against the wall, and none of them knew anything—nothing."

Gus frowned. "Did they say anything that could help us figure out where they're from?"

"Nothing," said Gugi. "They only talked about getting back what belonged to them; said they were through making money for whitey. Believe me, I wish I could help. If you find them just call me—before the dime goes down, I'll be there and I'll kill them with my bare hands. I'll . . ." Gugi was speechless. "Ah, *madonna me*," he said quietly now, looking toward the ceiling, "you can have my soul if you just let me find them," he vowed. He turned toward them. "The kid is still scared. Whenever he sees a *tutzone* on the street he grabs my hand—I feel like stomping every nigger I see."

Gus nodded. "Okay," he said, "thanks a lot."

"Thanks," said the young man. He didn't shake hands with Gugi as he left.

"Yeah, I paid them twenty-five thousand," said Abe Handleman, the little man with bald head and close-set eyes sitting across from Tony.

After Tony had finished with Big Diamond, he had called Gianni, who told him to continue uptown to the Inwood section and stop at the Holiday Lounge, another bar, and talk to someone Gianni called Jerry the Jew. Tony followed instructions, and located him, a rather tall man with lacquered fingernails and a pinky ring who puffed a big cigar. Jerry the Jew advised Tony that some *schwarzes* had snatched Mike Wallace, one of his key bankers, about a week ago and dumped him in the river just last night. He also told Tony where he could find Abe Handleman, Mike Wallace's partner.

"How much ransom did they want?" Tony asked Handleman. He peered over his cup of coffee at the little man who looked more like the corner news dealer than a rackets man.

"They wanted fifty. I told them I liked my partner, but not that much . . ."

"What happened?"

"I *hondled* with them. I told them I only had fifteen. Give us forty, they said. Twenty. Thirty-five. I finally told them: look, if my arms fall off, not another penny—even if they kill him and me together, not another penny more than twenty-five. They took it."

"How long did they let you *hondle*?" asked Tony, putting down his coffee.

"They were anxious, but not so anxious that they'd blow the money. It took a couple days," said Handleman.

"Were they tough? What was your impression?"

"They killed my partner—I guess they were tough enough for that, no?"

Tony studied the little man. "How many of them were there?"

"I only spoke to one, the same one all the time. A real *schwarze* voice, too. He was hungry for the money, believe me. When it came to the payoff I didn't see them, so I couldn't tell you how many."

"You deal with niggers—are any of them hustling numbers for you?" Tony pressed.

"Yeah. We work Harlem, 135th-155th. You got to have *schwarzes* work for you there."

"And you don't know who could be involved in this?"

"If it's any of our boys I don't know it—if I knew it'd be different."

"How did they arrange to give your partner back?"

"When I got the money together, they called me again. I didn't know where from. I told them I wanted to speak to Mike. They said okay and I spoke to him last night, at about twelve. At least I *thought* I spoke to him."

"He was already croaked by then," said Tony.

Handleman nodded. "They must have played a recording so I'd give them the dough."

"And you have no idea who they can be?"

"If I knew, would I be sitting here while they spend my money? I mean, we got our boys too—especially when they sell me a dead body. All I can tell you is they knew us—they knew the operation. But exactly who they are, I haven't any idea. If you find out, let me know; maybe I can get a little satisfaction for my twenty-five thousand."

"I'll let you know," said Tony. "Where did you make the payoff?"

"At the Cloisters—that museum on the hill," he said, seeing Tony's frown. "There's an old castle up there. They told me to come up the main road so they'd see if anyone was with me. Halfway up, this *schwarze* comes out of the dark and puts his hand up like a traffic cop. Only he's got a black mask like the Lone Ranger. There he was, the black Lone Ranger. So, I stop. He takes the money. Tells me to keep going up the road while they count the money, and if it's all there my partner will be standing in the road when I come back down. I go up, I come down—but there's no one there, no *schwarze*, no partner, nothing. *Drek*. Do you understand *drek*?"

"I know *drek:* shit," said Tony flatly.

"You got a *yiddishe kopf*."

"I've got an Italian head," Tony said. "You didn't recognize anyone? You can't tell me anything else, not even what kind of car they had?"

"What can I tell you? A *schwarze* Lone Ranger comes out of the dark and disappears and that's all I know. Except the son of a bitch killed my partner and kept my twenty-five thousand."

7:30 P.M.

Gianni sat at the desk in the garage office, smoking a cigarette. Frankie the Pig sat next to him. The other men were ranged about the small office, listening and smoking, leaning against the walls and counters.

"All right, let's see what we have," Gianni said. "So far, we know there's been one kidnaping and one almost-kidnaping where they were paid off for Gugi's grandson without having to snatch anyone. And we know colored men were involved in both incidents. We also know both victims had something to do with the rackets in Harlem or the black sections of the Bronx. But that's about all we know—not much to go on."

"Except that they must be real shit," said Frankie the Pig. "They don't respect anything, even little kids. They'd kill Sal as soon as look at him." He gazed back at Gianni. "When these guys call tonight, what are we going to do?"

"Talk to them. See what's on their minds. See how much they want."

"We better give them what they want," said Frankie the Pig. "These crazy bastards'll get tired of keeping Sal alive, and they'll croak him."

"Not too fast," said Gianni. "They'll only think about killing Sal after they're sure we're going to come through with the money. But we're not going to take a recording—we'll need real proof that Sal is alive, and that he's still alive at the payoff. That'll take time to arrange, and it gives us more time to track them down."

"How can we make them give us proof?" asked Tony.

"We'll have to figure that out," Gianni replied.

"I'm for making the deal as soon as we can—tonight. Let's not chance it," said Frankie the Pig. "Let's arrange the payoff someplace we can get to first and rig it out so we grab these *tutzone* bastards."

"I realize we're not dealing with Einsteins," said Gianni, "but they're not going to get suckered into a trap."

"Let's do it fast," said Gus. "Let's try and grab them."

"Yeah, let's get them," Bobby Matteawan hissed.

Gianni shook his head. "We have to assume they're not going to let themselves be trapped. We have to figure it their way and beat them at their own game. If we force it, they may kill Sal."

Frankie the Pig frowned. "What are we going to do?" he said, "let them make suckers out of us?" He looked around.

"I'm not worrying about us right now—only about Sal," Gianni shot back. He looked directly into Frankie the Pig's eyes.

Frankie the Pig nodded.

"Now, how much money do we have?" asked Gianni.

"We can put together about twenty without any problem," said Frankie the Pig.

"What will you do with that, give them a down payment?"

"What do you mean?"

"You think they'll let you get away that easy when they got twenty-five for some nickel-and-dime hood uptown, and fifty from a broken-down hobo in the Bronx?"

"That's what we've got and if they don't like it, they can fuck themselves," said Frankie the Pig quickly.

Gianni kept silent. He puffed his cigarette and blew out a stream of smoke. It lofted up, drifting toward the wall and a calendar picturing a naked girl. The smoke bounced off the calendar softly.

"And that's the final word?" Gianni asked them. "Anything over 20,000 and they can fuck themselves? And Sal?"

The others looked around.

Tony's thin lips pursed, his eyes hot with anger. "If a creep junkie in the Bronx can pay fifty thousand, what are we, pikers?"

"He wasn't a junkie; he was a dealer," said Gus.

"It's all the same shit to me," said Tony. "Well?" He glared at them in turn, his steely eyes resting on Frankie the Pig.

"Why are you looking at me like that?" said Frankie.

"Why do you think? You're second man here—what are you boss of, a bunch of pikers?"

Frankie the Pig's jaw muscles flexed. He turned to Gianni. "How much do you figure?"

"Maybe seventy-five."

"*Seventy-five*? How the hell are we going to come up with that?"

"You mean Sal's not worth it?" said Joey. "Haven't we all made bread for our kids' mouths with Sal? Hasn't he always been a stand-up guy? We're talking about his life, not *a boost*for his daughter's wedding."

"Sure he's worth it," said Gus, "but it's still a lot of dough to come up with just like that." He snapped his fingers.

"We've all got our boys in the street," said Tony; "everybody'll have to dig in. And we've got plenty of other people who owe us—let them kick in too. We're always there when they need something."

"We don't need any charity," said Frankie the Pig.

"What charity?" said Tony. "It's our money—we'll get it back in circulation as soon as we get Sal back."

"That's the idea," said Gianni. "Sal's men won't let him down. Certainly I won't let him down. Get everybody who owes you money and have them collect in advance, Frankie—make them come up with it right now."

"Okay. We'll get all the money we need. Otherwise there'll be some broken heads. Now listen," Frankie said. "Get everybody out there working. We'll take care of the big bosses ourselves; let your boys talk to everybody in the street.

"Okay?" he asked, looking at Gianni.

Gianni nodded. "Once we have that solved, at least we'll know we can make whatever ransom they ask."

"But we're not going to stand still and be taken like suckers," said Tony.

"Of course not," said Gianni. "But right now they have a little edge on us, don't you think? We'll bargain with them. But if they put their foot down at some point we'll have to play it like suckers, or we're going to find Sal thrown in front of the restaurant."

Their eyes showed they were thinking of the night before.

"We can't get it all together tonight, Gianni," said Frankie the Pig.

"Of course not," said Gianni. "I don't even want you to. The fact that we have to collect it gives us some time to maneuver and try to locate them meanwhile."

"When we find them, when we find them . . ." said Frankie, opening his palms, starting to work up steam.

"Relax, Frankie," said Gianni. "We have work to do."

"Well how are we going to find them? You said yourself we have nothing to go on."

"We haven't *much* to go on," said Gianni. "We know they must be connected with narcotics or numbers. And they know the setup of a couple of mobs—they knew who'd have money and how to get at them. If we had time we could trace every contact of the people they kidnaped—their suppliers, messengers, runners, customers—and that's where we'd find them."

Tony nodded. "Let's go out and do it. Let's get all those people in here."

"We don't have that much time," said Gianni. "We'll have to do it later. Don't worry—We're narrowing the gap on them right this minute; we just have to keep working at it."

The garage door opened. It was Angie the Kid, his collar up around his ears, his hat brim pulled down tight. He shook the rain off himself.

"Did you find anything?" asked Gianni.

"Did I! I found that guy in the Bronx that was kidnaped. They took him to an apartment and kept him two days, then let him go after his people paid thirty-five thousand."

"They kept him two days?" asked Gianni.

"Yeah," replied Angie the Kid, excited at his own discovery.

"Colored men?"

"Right."

"Does he know where he was kept?"

"Somewhere in Queens, he figures," replied Angie, billowing with pride.

"Where is he—did you bring him back with you?"

Angie the Kid gaped at Gianni, his pride subsiding. "No."

"Why not, you dummy," said Frankie the Pig.

"Take it easy, Frankie," said Gianni, "Angie's done fine. He's gotten us closer to this than anyone else. Angie, jump in your car. Go get this man and bring him back as soon as you can. Gus, go with him."

"Sure, Gianni, sure," said Angie the Kid. "I'm sorry. I didn't think we'd want him around."

"You did well, Angie," said Gianni. "Now go get him."

"Okay, Gianni." Angie the Kid pulled his collar up around his ears and went outside again. Gus put on his coat and followed.

Frankie the Pig stared after them angrily.

"He's all right," said Gianni; "just young. It'll be all right. Besides, we have thinking to do now."

The phone rang. They looked at it. Gianni let it ring again before his hand went to the receiver.

"Hello?" said a woman's voice on the other end. "How late is your kitchen open tonight?"

Gianni shrugged. "Until about 9:30, madam."

"Do you have *pasta fazool* on the menu tonight?"

"If we don't we'll make it specially for you."

Bobby Matteawan began to laugh. Frankie turned; Bobby quieted, glaring back at him.

"How come someone called the booth instead of the listed phone in back?" asked Tony.

"Because Mike has both numbers on his matches," said Frankie the Pig.

The phone rang again.

"If it's a customer tell him we're closed," said Bobby Matteawan.

"Hello," said Gianni.

"We called last night about Sal. Is Frankie the Pig there?" said the voice on the other end.

"I've been waiting for your call," said Gianni. "Frankie asked me to talk to you."

"Who are you, man?"

"I'm the one you want to talk to."

"I want to talk to the man in charge," said the voice.

"Then start talking," said Gianni.

"Okay, man, I'll talk business. The business is Sal. You know Sal?"

"I know Sal. What about him?"

"Who are you, man? I mean, I don't want to waste my time with just nobody."

"I'm the one you want to talk to, so talk. If we've got business, let's do it." Gianni was cold and precise.

"We want a hundred thousand," said the voice.

"A hundred's a lot of money," Gianni said, so the others would know.

Frankie the Pig stood suddenly, his face twitching with anger. He reached out for the phone.

Gianni rose quickly, his eyes burning into Frankie's face. He put his hand over the receiver: "*Sit down, or I swear you'll never walk out of this place alive.*"

Gianni looked around. Tony jumped off the counter, his body tensed, waiting for the word. Frankie the Pig's hand stayed in midair.

"It ain't so much when you figure it's going to buy a friend's life," said the voice. "That's the price."

"It'll take time. I don't know how much we can put together," said Gianni. "After all, this is the first we know of it. We're not in narcotics so we don't have a lot of cash around."

"We know what you guys are into," said the voice. "We know for too long. That's over now, baby. You can get the money. And you better get it. We'll call again tomorrow night. Same time, same place. Be ready to move."

"We don't want back a dead man," said Gianni. "We've got to be sure our man's alive."

"You get the bread, you're not going to get a dead man. Cross us, and he'll be deader than dead. And don't think you can string this out. Tomorrow at eight." The phone on the other end went dead.

8:45 P.M.

Lieutenant Schmidt pulled the earphones away from his ears and slipped them off his head. He looked at Quinn and Feigin. They were standing in the room, their listening post in P.S. 21.

"Well, we got a kidnaping all right," said Schmidt.

Feigin wound the recorded tape back onto the spool. "But *who* kidnaped Sal?"

"The answer to that'll get you the cigar," said Quinn.

"The only thing we know for sure is that Sal Angeletti was snatched by a jigaboo," said Schmidt. "Other than that, we're in the dark."

"You mean, in the darkie," said Quinn. He lit the small stub of a cigar that he had been alternately chewing and smoking for the last hour.

"That's very cute," said Schmidt. "If you were as clever as you're cute, maybe you could find out who's behind this."

"What do you want us to do, Lou?" asked Feigin.

"We can try questioning those mugs down at the Two Steps Down Inn," Quinn suggested.

"They'll clam up like nothing happened," said Feigin.

"Not only that, we'll blow our cover to boot," said Schmidt. "The minute we show up they'll figure out pretty fast that we have the restaurant tapped." He thought a moment. "Still, it won't make any difference—they can't very well yank this wire or the colored guys won't be able to call them and they might get Sal killed."

"That's right on target," said Feigin.

"I wonder who's on this end of the phone. Either of you recognize his voice?" asked Schmidt.

Quinn shook his head.

Feigin finished installing a new tape in the recorder and put the voice tape in an envelope. "Must be Gianni Aquilino. Didn't Compagna's man Sonny call him today, asking about Matteawan?"

"That's right," said Schmidt. "This is big now, with Aquilino and Compagna in it. We better stay close."

"You want us to go down and pull them in, Lou?" asked Quinn.

"Not just yet. I don't want them to start covering their tracks until we have as much information as we can get. First thing I want is for one of you to call Central Intelligence and see if anything else like this has been happening around town. Sounds to me as if they've already made a couple of snatches. The guy fished out of the river this morning might have been one of them."

"I'll get on that," said Quinn.

"Jack, you call communications. Have them put a tap on Angeletti's phone."

"We already got that, Lou."

"Not at the joint; try one on his house. Maybe we can pick up something coming in or out of there."

"I don't think the colored guys would be calling there," said Quinn.

"I don't expect them to," said Schmidt; "but we've got to follow the victim to get the collar."

"And if we don't act fast, we'll have a murder on our hands," said Feigin. "Either the jigs'll murder Sal, or these wops'll start shooting holes in everybody in sight."

"All right. Let's get on it," said Schmidt. "Tomorrow morning maybe we'll see what they're willing to tell us by themselves. When they wire Angeletti's apartment, Quinny, have the machine put in here with this one. If you need another, use the one in the office for the time being."

"Okay, Lou."

The three men left the room and the custodian let them out of the school.

10:00 P.M.

Angie the Kid and Gus entered the garage. With them was a thin man with a hooked nose and dark, close-set eyes.

"This is Carmelo Bianci," said Angie, "the guy I told you about." He was relieved now, his face showing the strain he had been enduring as he had gone to fetch him. Gus entered the office and stood to the side.

"Hello," said Gianni, extending his hand.

Bianci looked at Gianni with eyes that remembered the old days. He stood stiffly, just staring. His hand reached out blindly.

"Sit down," said Gianni.

Frankie the Pig rose and put out a chair for him directly in front of the desk. He studied Bianci. Angie the Kid leaned against the counter next to Gus.

"Just call me Mickey," said Bianci, still standing.

"Okay, Mickey," said Gianni, pointing him to the chair. "I understand you were kidnaped."

"I sure was," said Mickey, "by some *mulanyoms*. I'm telling you, they scared the shit out of me. Like I told Angie here, they come and grab me in the place where I hang out, you know?"

"We don't know, Mickey," said Gianni. "What place is that?"

"I'm at this place, the Fireside, over in the Bronx. It's a bar. Not a bad joint."

"Go on," said Gianni.

"Well, like I said," Mickey continued, smiling a little at them, "I hang out in this joint. I use it like an office."

"What racket are you in?" asked Frankie the Pig.

"A little of everything," he shrugged; "wherever I can earn."

"Are you in drugs?" asked Gianni.

"Some. You know, a lot of guys—girls too, but I don't like to fool around with them—a lot of guys want the stuff. What the hell, you know?"

"You deal with coloreds?" asked Gianni.

"Sure, they buy it. They ain't got much money, though, except Friday and Saturday. But there's volume, so it makes up for it."

Gianni studied Mickey silently. Frankie the Pig's face was streaked with displeasure.

"You know Gugi?" asked Gianni.

"Sure. He's in the same racket, but he's up further. I'm in the southeast Bronx and he's up around Boston Road."

"You have any coloreds working for you?"

"Some, sure. Oh, I know what you're getting at—but I haven't come up with anything. I can't link it to nobody I know."

"All right," said Gianni. "Tell us about how you were snatched. What happened?"

"It was about a week ago, let's see," he said, looking at the ceiling. "What's today?"

"Tuesday," said Angie the Kid.

"Tuesday, right. Well, it was like Friday before last Tuesday. Ten days ago. I was in the joint, ready for a night's work. I was just hanging around. And some guy says there's a call on the phone. So I walk up to the booth, and there's this spook inside—I couldn't hardly even see him. I figured he was using the phone. But he turns to me, and he's got this knife, you know? I seen it shine. I didn't figure it was a snatch or anything. I thought maybe a heist for a bag—and I'd give the guy the bag if he wanted it that bad. So I move back, kind of, and I bunk into this guy standing right behind me. I just turned my head a bit, like this—" Mickey demonstrated.

"Go on," said Gianni. Tony drifted in and stood opposite Angie the Kid and Gus.

"I didn't even hear this guy get behind me. But I turned my head, and it's another spook. So I know I got trouble now. The bartender's got a gun, at the bar, but he's further down, in the back of the joint. I'm thinking, maybe I'll call the barkeep for help, but then I figure this guy with the knife looks like he knows how to stick it in my gut."

"What did he say?" Gianni said.

"I was mostly looking at the knife. But the guy behind me says, 'Come outside.' The other guy moves the knife to my throat. I ain't arguing with him. The guy behind me is almost up my ass, he's so close. We walk outside and there's another guy in a car."

"What kind of car?" said Gianni.

"Some kind of beat-up job, maybe a Ford or something. It was real beat-up."

"They probably used some junkbox on purpose so it couldn't be identified," Gianni said to the others.

"I bet it's their own car. They're not smart enough to think of that," said Tony.

"Let's not make a mistake and sell them short. Go ahead," Gianni said, turning back to Mickey.

"I get in this beat-up car and the guy behind me gets into the back seat with me. The guy with the knife gets in the front, hanging the knife down behind the front seat so the people in the street can't see it. But I can see it, you know? The guy in the back ties this rag around my eyes and then stuffs me down on the floor. The bastards, they got me rolled up like I was a ball."

"What did they look like?" asked Gianni.

"That's hard for me to say, you know. I mean, I know a lot of *yoms*, I deal with them all the time, them and spics, so I get to know what they look like. They don't really all look alike, you know? They're almost like we are—I mean they all got dark eyes and dark hair. But each guy looks different anyway."

"I know that, Mickey," said Gianni. "What did these look like?"

"Like I said, that's kind of tough to say, 'cause these guys were all wearing real dark shades and hats. A lot of these colored guys wear shades, so that don't look suspicious when they come in the joint, I guess. I couldn't get to see much of them when they grabbed me. During the ride, of course, I couldn't see a thing."

"How long did they drive you?"

"Maybe half an hour, forty-five minutes. We really had a ride."

"Do you know where they took you?"

"It must have been Queens. Yeah, it must have been. I mean, we went across a bridge—I could hear the tires making that noise when you go over a bridge. And then, later, while I was in the apartment where they kept me, I heard planes all the time—low, too. I could hear the engines like they were taking off, or coming in for a landing."

"Fine," said Gianni. "When you were in this apartment, were you blindfolded?"

"No, but the blinds were pulled down all the time. They wouldn't let me near the windows, so I couldn't see outside."

"How about the men who snatched you?" said Frankie the Pig. "Could you see them then?"

"They were two different guys. A little guy, his name was Hartfield, or Hartley, or something. They tried not to let me know their names. They'd call each other 'man,' and kept reminding each other not to use names. But one of them slipped once, he called the other guy Hartfield or Hartley, something like that."

"And the other?" said Gianni.

"I didn't catch his name. But he was a mean-looking bastard. The other guy, he was small, dark-skinned, with a mustache. The mean-looking bastard had a mustache too, but he was taller. He was pretty dark-skinned too."

"Did you notice anything about the apartment?" asked Gianni.

"I know it wasn't their apartment," said Mickey.

"How do you know that?"

"I heard them talking about some dame who was away for the weekend or something. There was pictures on the wall, a lot of pictures. And one dame was in most of them; I think it must have been her apartment."

"What did she look like? Did you recognize her?"

"No, I didn't recognize her," said Mickey. "But she must have been one of those bunnies, you know?"

"A what?" said Frankie the Pig.

"A bunny, you know, like in that *Playboy* magazine, with the ears and the thing on her ass," said Mickey.

"Was she white?" Gianni asked.

"No, she was colored too."

"A chocolate bunny," Tony said, caustically.

"She was a good-looking head, this dame. She didn't have them nigger features, you know. She was light, good looking, long hair."

Gianni's eyes widened. "A bunny from the Playboy Club, colored. There's a piece of real information. You sure it was the Playboy Club?"

"I couldn't tell exactly from the picture, but it looked like it."

"Was there anything else in the apartment from the Playboy Club?" Gianni pressed him.

Mickey thought for a moment, looking at the ceiling. "Yeah, there was an ashtray. I was smoking a lot. *Minca*, I was nervous. I didn't know if these guys were going to croak me, or what? If it was up to this taller guy, the mean bastard, they would have. But the little guy was all right."

"The ashtray was from the Playboy Club?" said Gianni.

"Yeah, I'm sure of that," said Mickey.

"Fine. What else happened?"

"Well, I didn't exactly know. I was in the apartment, and the guys who brought me there must have been talking with my people to get the dough."

"How much did they get?" asked Frankie.

"They took us for thirty-five large," he said proudly.

"How did you get back?" said Gianni.

"The same way. In the back of the car, blindfolded. They left me in the parking lot over at La Guardia. It was late at night and the joint was deserted. They just tossed me out, blindfolded still. They took off fast. I didn't even take the mask off. I just stood there for a while. When I didn't hear the car no more, I took the thing off my eyes. I seen some headlights coming at me and I thought the bastards were coming back to run me over. I started to move—you know, this way and that, zigzag like. But it was my own guys. They called to me, 'Mickey, Mickey, it's us.' And I got in, and that was it."

"Would you be able to recognize them again, those five men?" said Gianni.

"The two guys in the apartment, for sure. The other guys, no. Only that there's two of them big guys, and the third one is shorter and wide, built like a bull. I been looking for them myself, but who's going to see them again?"

"What kind of house was it?" asked Gianni.

"We've even put up some money for information—ten Gs. But nobody's come up with anything. What do you mean, what kind of house?"

"Big, little, new, old?"

"I couldn't tell you. We walked up and down a couple of flights, but I don't know if it was a big house, you know, an apartment house or what. But it wasn't too old—I mean it wasn't one of those slum kind of buildings. Inside, the apartment was all right: a nice joint, to tell you the truth."

"Anything else that might be helpful, Mickey?" said Gianni.

He shook his head. "Not that I can think of. One of your guys got snatched too?"

"We've got a similar problem, Mickey," said Gianni. "I appreciate your help."

"It's nothing, Gianni. If there's anything else I can do, just call."

"I will, thanks," said Gianni. "Angie, give Mickey a ride back to his place."

Angie nodded and moved toward the door. Mickey stood and shook hands with Gianni and Frankie. He followed Angie out of the garage.

"Well," said Gianni. "We've got something really real now."

"The bunny?" asked Frankie the Pig.

Gianni nodded. "Right. We've got to find a chocolate bunny."

"I didn't even know they had any," said Tony.

"Now you know," said Gus.

"You want me to go up to that Playboy place and look around, Gianni?" asked Tony.

"Yes."

"Take Gus with you," said Frankie the Pig. "If you took Matteawan he'd end up playing around with the dames and we wouldn't see him for two days."

"Yeah. And you can't come either," said Tony, a cool smile on his lips.

"*Minca*. That reminds me, I better call *a cummad'* and tell her I'm busy," said Frankie the Pig. "I hope we find Sal soon."

"I do too," said Gianni.

WEDNESDAY, FEBRUARY 10

10:00 A.M.

JOHN FEIGIN WAS SLEEPILY LEAFING through the September issue of *Reader's Digest* he had found in the school custodian's office. During the night, until the restaurant closed, there was very little action, nothing significant, on the phone-booth tap. There was nothing at all on Sal Angeletti's home. Communications had completed that installation about 1:00 A.M.

It was just about time for one of the other detectives from the squad to relieve him, Feigin thought, looking at his watch. He suddenly noticed the recorder on the tap at Angeletti's home moving, the spool of tape winding. Feigin picked up the headset and fit the cups over his ears.

"Hello, Maria?" Feigin heard a woman's voice from the outside line.

"Oh, hello Andrea," said the voice in Sal's home.

"What's the matter?" Andrea asked, "you don't sound well."

"I didn't sleep last night," said Maria. "Sal hasn't been home now in two nights. How could I sleep?"

"He hasn't been home in two nights?"

"Two nights. He was out Monday night and didn't even tell me. And I fixed veal and peppers—the way I do? And he didn't even come home. So I figured I'd put it in the refrigerator and he'd eat it Tuesday. But he didn't come home last night again."

"Maybe he heard you kept the leftovers."

"It isn't funny, sister of mine," said Maria soberly.

"What do you think?"

"What can I think? I haven't any idea," said Maria. "When he gets tied up like this, usually he lets me know—he sends Joey over, or Tony."

"Nobody came over to explain anything?"

"Gianni Aquilino came over just now."

"Gianni Aquilino?" Andrea was surprised.

"Just like that," said Maria. "Gianni rang the doorbell and came in for coffee. I haven't seen him it must be three years."

"How did he look, still as handsome as ever?"

"Still the same—elegant, handsome."

Feigin on the earphones was listening and taking notes. He had written the name Gianni Aquilino, underscoring it three times.

"Remember when he was sweet on me?" asked Andrea.

"Remember the lions eating the Christians?"

"Speak for yourself, sister dear."

"We're both old now," said Maria.

Andrea sighed. "What did Gianni say?"

"He said he was in the neighborhood, and he knew Sal wasn't home, so he thought he'd come and say hello and let me know Sal was all right."

"That was nice of him," said Andrea.

"Gianni is considerate," said Maria. "Not like that Sal, leaving me alone without calling."

"Sal was always that way—you expect him to change now?"

"Well, it was nice of Gianni to come over and let me know everything is okay."

"Yes," said Andrea. "How are things otherwise?"

"Okay, and you?"

"Okay," said Andrea. "Except for Jimmy's ulcer."

"How are the children?"

"Okay. Everybody's fine. Well, I just called to see how you were. Let me know about Sal, if he's okay?"

"I will. Thanks for calling."

"You're welcome. Remember, it's your turn now," said Andrea.

"How could I forget it?"

They both laughed and hung up.

Feigin opened the door, locked it behind him and went down to the principal's office to call the precinct house. A few children were walking through the halls, toward their classrooms, or to lavatories. They looked at him quickly as they passed, wondering who the new teacher was.

"Hey, Lou, I got something interesting over here," said Feigin into the telephone.

"What's that?"

Feigin glanced at the principal's secretary, who was now listening to the conversation. She looked down at her typewriter.

"Hold it," Feigin said in the phone. "Miss, is there a private office I can use?" He looked at her without hiding his contempt. She was a little Jew intellectual, he thought, one of those liberals.

"You can go into the principal's office," she said, pointing to an inner door.

"Thanks. Hold it, Lou," said Feigin, pushing the HOLD button. He walked into the office and picked up the phone. "Listen, Lou. Gianni Aquilino was just over to see Sal's wife."

"Aquilino? I didn't think he'd be around this morning."

"He went over to tell her that Sal's all right," said Feigin. "He must have been the guy talking on the phone last night."

"Of course. Who else would talk instead of Frankie?" said Schmidt. "Very good."

"I thought you'd like to know right away."

"I think we should drop over there and pick Gianni up," said Schmidt. "Maybe he's used to the soft life these days. Maybe he'll talk where the others won't."

"You want me to pick him up?" asked Feigin.

"No, I'll take care of it from here," said Schmidt. "You stay on the wires until I get somebody over to relieve you. Then come in. Aquilino will be here by the time you get here."

"If his high-priced lawyer doesn't get there first."

"I'll see you in a bit." Schmidt hung up.

Feigin went out of the office and returned to his listening post. The tape in Sal's house was going again. Feigin donned his headset quickly.

"Even so, he's still your father," Maria's voice was saying.

"But that doesn't mean I have to agree with what he is or does," said a female voice. "One of these days you're going to be a widow. He thinks he's still a kid."

"He's got a lot more life than a lot of men," said Maria.

"And if he'll just stop what he's doing and retire, and go to Florida, he'll keep that life, God willing, for a long time. I just worry about him, mother."

"I know. I do too," Maria agreed. "But what can we do? You can't teach an old dog new tricks. That's the way he is."

"I'm sure Daddy's all right. Didn't Gianni say so?"

"Yes, but even so, how does Gianni know? He's not around to know from day to day."

"If Gianni Aquilino says everything is okay, mother, I'm sure it is."

"You think so?"

"I know so. And so do you."

"I guess you're right," said Maria. "It's just that I worry."

"Do you want me to come over and stay with you today?"

"Can you?"

"Sure. I'll bundle up little Sal and we'll come over and spend the day together."

"That'll be nice," said Maria. "I'll fix some food the way you like it."

"We'll be there in about forty-five minutes."

"Okay. And bundle Sal up warm, now. It's cold out."

"Yes, mother."

"All right, come on, we'll watch the astronauts on the TV. Tell little Sal to hurry to Nonna."

"Okay, good-by."

"Good-by."

Feigin shrugged, picking up his *Reader's Digest* again.

10:30 A.M.

Gianni lit a cigarette and put the lighter back in his pocket. He was sitting to the right of Lieutenant Schmidt's desk. He smiled at him. "You're really looking great, lieutenant. And the promotion, that's great. Couldn't have happened to a nicer guy. How long has it been since I've seen you?"

"Come on, Gianni, don't horse around," Schmidt said patiently.

"I'm not horsing around," said Gianni. "I'm delighted you made lieutenant. It's nice to know the old-timers on top are letting in a few besides their own for the promotions."

Schmidt leaned back in his chair and smiled. "You look great too, Gianni. Come on now, level with me. We're not trying to pin anything on you, or on Sal. You know-that. We know there's something wrong. We're trying to help—but you've got to cooperate."

"You know, I wish there was something for me to tell you, lieutenant. But I don't know what in blazes you're talking about. As far as I know, there's nothing wrong."

"Then where's Sal?"

"He must be at home," Gianni replied calmly.

"You know he's not at home. We know he's got troubles and we can help."

"You know more than I do, lieutenant. I don't know about any trouble. By the way, did you get in touch with my lawyer?" Gianni said, turning around. Feigin and Quinn were standing in the doorway.

The lieutenant looked up at his two detectives.

"We called him. Luca said he'd be over in about a half hour," said Quinn. "That was twenty minutes ago."

"That's fine. Do you know Sandro Luca, lieutenant?"

"No, I don't think so."

"A nice kid. A terrific lawyer too. He's going places. You'll like him. He's a real gentleman."

"That's great, Gianni," said Schmidt. "But you didn't need your attorney."

"I know, I know, but that's what he's paid for. I may as well get my money's worth." Gianni smiled, puffing slowly on his cigarette.

"Gianni, believe me, we're trying to help. This has nothing to do with you or anyone else you know."

"I believe you, and I think you guys are doing great work. I mean that. You're trying to help out a private citizen in distress, no matter what his past, or if you like or dislike him. It's great. But as I said, I don't know what you're talking about."

"I don't want to get rough on you, Gianni," said Schmidt.

"I don't want you to either. I'm too old for that kind of thing. And you said I didn't need my lawyer."

"You know you could be held for obstructing justice."

"What obstruction, lieutenant? What's the crime we're talking about?"

"You know what we're talking about," Feigin said.

"You know more than I do, then," said Gianni, not turning. "I may have been out of circulation a long time, lieutenant, but you know you can't hold me. Just let's understand each other. I don't know what's going on. As a matter of fact, when I leave here, I'm going to call Sal and find out if there's anything wrong."

Another detective came to the doorway. "Lieutenant, there's a lawyer here asking about Gianni Aquilino."

"You're going to like him," said Gianni.

Schmidt nodded. "Show him in."

"Good morning, lieutenant," said Sandro, entering the office. He shook hands with him and Gianni. Then Schmidt introduced Feigin and Quinn. "Is Mr. Aquilino being held on a crime of some sort?"

"No, we're investigating what we believe is a crime perpetrated against a friend of his. We can't help if we don't get cooperation from the victim's friends."

Sandro looked at Gianni. "May I speak to my client alone for a moment, lieutenant?"

"I don't think that's necessary," said Schmidt, "not just yet."

"See how we disagree. I think it is necessary. And of course a person accused of a crime can confer with his attorney."

"I guess I didn't make myself clear," said Schmidt. "Aquilino is not being charged with a crime."

"In that case, we don't have to stay here any longer, do we?"

The lieutenant stared at Sandro, then at Gianni. He shrugged. "Listen, we're trying to help. If you don't want help, that's your business. If Angeletti ends up a stiff, don't come crying around here."

"Lieutenant, I'd help you if I could," said Gianni. "Seriously."

"Yeah, I bet," said Schmidt. "Okay. Take off."

Gianni rose and moved toward the door. Sandro followed him.

"Take care of yourself now, lieutenant," said Gianni. "Good seeing you again."

Schmidt just nodded, a frown souring his face.

Sandro followed Gianni down the steps to the first floor, past the front desk, and out the large wooden doors to the street.

"Let's go over to the Grotta Azzura," said Gianni. "They picked me up just before breakfast. Now it's almost time for lunch."

The two men walked to Broome Street, and west to the restaurant. They descended the steep steps and entered a large room, brightly lit, with white tile floor, and stuffed game fish on the walls. In the back there was an open kitchen where the chefs in the white hats were vociferously talking in Italian as they moved among the hanging copper pots. The owner recognized Gianni and smiled. He seated them at a table on the side and took their order. Most of the other tables were still empty.

"Now, what is this all about, Gianni?" asked Sandro.

"We've had some trouble," said Gianni. "Sal was kidnaped and we're in the process of working something out with the kidnapers."

"Kidnaped?"

"That's right. And I can't tell the cops. I don't want them to mess anything up for us. The kidnapers have already killed one of their victims."

"That sounds incredible—who was it?"

"That's what we're trying to find out. But we haven't come up with anything substantial yet. Neither have the cops. They must have a tap on the phone at the Two Steps. That's where they got their information."

"Couldn't they have gotten it from someone on the shreet?"

"It's still too soon. No one knows it, not even Sal's wife. But what the hell can we do, we can't tear out the phone or the kidnapers won't be able to get in touch with us. The cops probably figured it that way too," Gianni smiled. "Now what will happen when I refuse to testify, even with the committee's immunity?"

"We'll be sent before a judge in the Supreme Court."

"And when we get to court."

"The judge'll order you to go back to the committee and testify. And if you refuse to testify after he orders you to, you'll be guilty of contempt of court, and they can put you in jail for thirty days."

"Still the same old bit," said Gianni. "Then they'll bring me back, and if I still refuse, I'll get another thirty days, and so on."

"That's about the size of it, Gianni. And that's just what they want to happen."

The waiter brought the antipasto.

"You know, Sandro, I can talk to you, not only because you're my lawyer, but because you've been close to me for so many years—since you were a kid—and your family, your uncle. I couldn't talk to the others. They're so hidebound by the old ways that if I told them some of the things I've been thinking, they'd believe I was getting soft. And if they believed that, I wouldn't be able to help Sal."

"You're not soft, Gianni. Perhaps you've changed your point of view in the last few years."

"Whatever it is, I realized it the other night when I was trying to keep the boys from flying off the handle. I was telling them that at this point, we're concerned only with getting Sal back. Afterward, we'd take the kidnapers and tear them apart. In the old days, that would have meant literally tearing someone apart—killing him. But as I was saying it the other night, I said to myself, *Gianni, you don't want to kill anyone, or even have anyone killed.* And you know, it was a strange feeling. I was rallying the troops, the words were there, but I didn't mean them."

"And you think there's something wrong with not wanting to kill people?"

"Sandro, they have offended Sal, me, all of us; they have done something for which they should be punished severely. But, well," he paused momentarily. "This is the first time I'm saying these things aloud to anyone in the world. This is strictly in confidence."

"Of course."

"Swear to me."

"I swear on the honor of my family, on the soul of Uncle Jim," Sandro said solemnly.

Gianni nodded. "I'm confused with these thoughts."

"Gianni, I know we'd all like to be Superman, and have all the answers, and never be confused. But Superman is only a comic strip."

Gianni smiled. "I understand that. Even so, it's hard. I haven't had to think of things like this for years, and now suddenly I find I'm no longer the same way I used to be. I don't think or feel the same way. But I still remember the old thoughts."

They were both silent.

"As long as we're exploring new thoughts, Gianni," Sandro said, "I have a new one for you, too."

"What's that?"

The waiter cleared away their plates, and brought the second course.

"I've been thinking about your refusing to testify, and going to jail for 30 or 60 days, and maybe then being indicted for contempt and going to jail for a year. Gianni, it's ridiculous."

Gianni studied Sandro carefully. "How come?"

"Because you could answer all their questions and have no worry about contempt or perjury or anything else."

"I don't get what you mean, Sandro. You know I can't testify to anything."

"That's just my point, Gianni. You say that automatically. Everybody's been saying it, over and over, for years. And then they go to jail for 30 days or a year. That's the old way. And I think that you, especially after what you've just told me, may be the one strong enough to change it."

"You know as well as I do, Sandro, that if I testify that I had lunch with someone on Sunday on the corner of 57th Street and that fellow comes in and says that he had lunch with me on Thursday on the corner of 57th Street, we both have troubles. The authorities want to get me, and everyone else, off the street. They're not concerned with substantial or technical grounds, good or bad methods. If I testify, I'm just opening the door to a lot of trouble. And if I open the door, who knows where the questions will go or stop?"

"Well, I've figured out there are only three areas about which you can be asked questions," said Sandro. "And none of them can cause you any trouble."

"Go on."

"One: they'll ask you about certain people you know—if you know Mario Siciliano, if you know Vito Giordano or this fellow or that. Now it's no crime just to know these people. The fact that you know someone is totally insignificant. Besides, the government already knows you know them."

"They already know everything," Gianni said.

"Fine. That helps to prove my point. If there was any significance to your just knowing these people, without proof of your planning a crime together or something, they would have arrested you for knowing them a long time ago."

Gianni nodded. "What's number two?"

"They'll ask you if you're a member of the Mafia or Cosa Nostra, or if you know what the Mafia or Cosa Nostra is."

"It doesn't even exist," Gianni said firmly.

"You mentioned that at the hearing, but you didn't finish the story," said Sandro.

"Sure there are Italians in rackets, Sandro. And Italian gangs," said Gianni. "It'd be ridiculous to say there aren't. But this thing about a syndicate, a national organization, is fantasy.

"You see," Gianni continued, "in Sicily a Mafia originated to protect the people from foreign kings who dominated and constantly plundered the land. Later on, the Mafiosi corrupted into brigands who began to exploit the people themselves. Some of these brigands came to America at the turn of the century and continued to terrorize their own people. I mean, how could they tell some Irishman to stick 'em up; they couldn't even speak English."

Sandro laughed, then waited while Gianni sipped his wine.

"But those old Mustache Petes turned seventy and retired in the early thirties. After them came the guys of my generation—came to the States as kids or born here of immigrant parents. We saw new ways of making money without breaking heads.

"Today, there's a new breed running things. They're totally American. And there's no more of that old Mafia. What the authorities call *Cosa Nostra* is just Italian gangs. There are all kinds of gangs in organized crime—Irish, Jewish, Negro—but Italians only trust Italians. We have our thing, *Cosa Nostra*."

"You're saying there's no syndicate?"

"I'm saying all the gangs are independent—no central leader, no central treasury, no national plan. It's free enterprise. Sure, the racket people know each other, just like lawyers or doctors, but they're not all partners."

"Then how do you explain the commission that's supposed to be in charge of everything?"

"When tough guys get angry, they can't go to court and get an injunction, or a restraining order. So they ask advice from other people in the same racket. And with so many suckers in the street, why should one tough guy fight another tough guy; it only wastes time and blood. This 'commission' is not a board giving orders, just guys keeping peace among themselves."

"That's just my point, Gianni. If there is no national organization, then why not testify and say so?"

"Go ahead, what's three?"

"Number three, they'll ask questions about specific crimes—did you plan this crime, did you commit that one."

"I didn't commit any crime," Gianni assured him.

"Well, tomorrow they'll give you immunity from prosecution in order to compel your testimony. If they had any information concerning any crime you did commit, they'd hardly give you immunity so they couldn't prosecute you. The fact is, they're giving you immunity because they have no information about specific crimes."

"There's no information because I haven't committed any."

"Fine. And those are the only areas about which you'll be asked. There'll be a lot of questions, but all in those areas. Isn't it ridiculous to go to jail because you refuse to answer those things?"

Gianni was pensive now, not speaking, as he returned to his food. "You know, Sandro," he said finally, "there's a lot to what you say. I guess this is the week for new things to be studied and explored. But what if I answer questions truthfully and other people come in and testify falsely or inaccurately? Then what will happen?"

"You'll have to tell everyone what you're doing. So they can guide themselves accordingly. They should all testify and throw the questions right back in the committee's face. No one has explained it to them before—but you could change it, Gianni. Do you know that the committee doesn't even want you to answer?"

"What do you mean?"

"They're up there putting on a show. And when witnesses take the Fifth and refuse to answer, the committee asks all kinds of questions which are only rumors and assumptions, even totally false. But they know the witnesses won't answer and this makes it seem as if their questions are true. The committee and the newspapers have a field day: you go to jail for thirty days, and the public has some adventure stories to read. But if you answered their questions honestly, you'd leave them with nothing."

"How about the others who've been subpoenaed? Won't they get in trouble because of me?"

"Gianni. Someone's got to open their eyes. When they see how easy it is for you to answer, maybe they'll stop going to jail needlessly too."

Gianni smiled at him. "It's tough just to say okay, I'll do it. What you say makes sense, but . . ."

"The others need your leadership. They have to be shown the way by someone with balls enough, frankly, to be the first one on the firing line. That's you, Gianni."

"There's an old saying for this," said Gianni. "*Il cavallo zoppo, si guardischi la via.*"

"What does that mean?"

"Very freely translated, it means the lame horse enjoys the road. It's the strong horse that has to break his back carrying the load through life."

"This is the only way it can be done, even if some of the others don't understand it at first."

"All right, come on now," said Gianni, signaling for a check. "I've got some work to do. I've sent men all over town trying to find information about Sal's kidnapers. We're even trying to find a colored bunny from the Playboy Club."

"How come?"

"She may know the kidnapers, or be one of their girlfriends."

"I know a colored bunny," said Sandro.

"You? How do you know a colored bunny?"

"I know one, Gianni. Does it matter how or why?"

"Does she live in Queens?" said Gianni.

"No, in Manhattan."

"How many colored bunnies are there?"

"Not too many. I don't go to the club, but I know some of the bunnies."

"This colored bunny of yours would know how many there are," said Gianni. "And probably know them pretty well, too."

"I imagine so," said Sandro.

"Do you know where to get in touch with her?"

Sandro took out a billfold from his inside jacket pocket and opened it. He took a small book from one of the compartments. "Here she is—Ginger."

Gianni watched Sandro, his eyes moving from the little book in Sandro's hand to Sandro's eyes. "You have her in your little address book? You know her that well?" The corners of Gianni's eyes crinkled as he smiled.

"Let's just say I know her," said Sandro.

"Okay. And let's just say you try and get in touch with her and find out who the other colored bunnies are, and where they live. It's important. We think that could lead us to the kidnapers."

"I'll go find her right now," said Sandro. "I'm sure she's still sleeping. She works until four in the morning."

"I'll be glad to send one of the fellows with you."

"I can handle it by myself."

"That's just what I'm afraid you'll do. And we need the information right away." Gianni smiled at him.

"I'll get it for you within the hour."

Gianni snatched the check from Sandro. After they reached the sidewalk, Sandro hailed a cab and headed uptown. Gianni walked slowly back to the garage, deep in thought.

1:15 P.M.

Sandro entered the tall brick building on First Avenue and 55th Street. He told the doorman he wanted to see Ginger North. The doorman picked up the intercom and rang apartment 34C. He waited, his ear to the phone, then shook his head.

"Ring it once more, please," Sandro said.

The doorman obliged, listening patiently. Suddenly, he nodded. "Hello, Mr.—" He looked at Sandro.

"Sandro."

"Mister Sandro to see you." He listened again. "Okay. Go right up. Apartment 34C."

Sandro took one of the elevators to the 34th floor. He walked to the C apartment and rang the bell. Ginger must have been waiting right behind the door; the peephole was moved, and instantly the door was opened for him.

Ginger was tall, five-foot-ten, tan-skinned, with almond eyes and long smooth black hair. A sheer shortie nightgown covered her only to the tops of her luscious legs. Beneath the lace Sandro could see her firm, dark-nippled breasts. She wore a sheer pair of bikini panties to match the top. Ginger was leaning against the wall just inside the door, her eyes half-closed with sleep. She was smiling at Sandro. Behind her, the apartment was dark.

"Come here, you," she said, reaching out as Sandro closed the door behind him. "I don't care why you're here, come on in and give me a squeeze." She put her arms around Sandro and held him closely.

Sandro circled her with his arms. "Hello, baby. I wake you up in the middle of your night, and you come out loving and hugging. Who in the world is as beautiful as you?"

"Nobody," she said softly, resting her head against his shoulder. "That's because you're my baby."

"And you're my baby," Sandro whispered.

"Come on and get in bed with me," Ginger whispered, her lips finding his neck, his lower ear.

"I just walk in the door, and you proposition me?"

"I can't stand up much longer," she said. "I've got to lie down. You might as well lie down with me."

"I need some information," said Sandro. "Really, serious stuff. I've got to ask you some questions first."

"Okay, okay. But ask them in bed. Come on." Ginger twisted around so that her arm was around Sandro's waist, and she walked toward the interior of the apartment. "Watch out for the cocktail table in front of the couch," she said. "I rearranged the place since the last time you were here. You rat."

"How can I see the cocktail table or the couch? It's pitch black in here."

"No ethnic remarks please." She guided Sandro across the thick pile rug, to the small bedroom on the far side of the living room. She slid down onto the large bed, pulling Sandro gently by the hand until he lay next to her. In the dark, he could smell the deep, passionate fragrance that always surrounded Ginger. She would never say what perfume it was, only that it was Ginger, impure and sinful, coming through her pores. The bed was king-size, and soft, with four pillows. Everything about Ginger was luxurious and soft.

"I'm still all dressed, in a suit and tie," Sandro said.

"I'll take care of that, lover." She struck a match. Sandro watched its course through the air, until it lit a candle on a night table beside the bed. Ginger propped a pillow behind her and began to unwork the knot in Sandro's tie.

"I really have to ask some questions," he said. "I'm sure you have some information I need."

"Ask away," said Ginger. She gently eased Sandro's arms out of his jacket. She stood and hung the jacket in her closet. As she stood in the candle flicker, Ginger raised the shortie nightgown over her head, exposing her taut, full breasts. They weren't huge, they were just beautiful. Ginger walked to Sandro's side of the bed, and standing directly in front of him as he sat wide-eyed, she began to unbutton his shirt.

"How the hell can I ask questions with you undressing me—the most beautiful goddamn woman in the world."

"Don't ask, then," she said, kissing Sandro's forehead, her breasts touching his face as she stood straight.

Sandro slipped his arms around her waist, pulling her closer.

"Uh, uh, let me finish with this shirt of yours." She pulled his shirt-tails out of his pants, and opened the cuff links. She eased it off his back. "Better hurry up with your questions. 'Cause when I finish this, I'm going to finish you, lover." She laughed at him.

Sandro smiled. The candle was scented, and a pungent, spicy fragrance wafted into the air.

"I want the names of the other colored bunnies, especially any who might live in Queens," said Sandro.

"Other chocolate bunnies," said Ginger pensively. She bent down and took off Sandro's left shoe.

"Oh, for Christ's sake," said Sandro. "I can take off the rest." He rose and slipped off his other shoe.

"There are only four of us now," said Ginger. "There were six, but two of them have been gone for a couple of months now."

"Any of them live in Queens?" asked Sandro.

"Let's see. There's Ann, Sandy, Jean and me."

"You we can forget about. You don't live in Queens."

"Right, dummy." She pushed him down to a sitting position again and worked at his pants, unsnapping them at the waist. "The others live in Manhattan—Ann by herself on 58th Street, just behind the Plaza; Sandy and Jean live on 74th Street and First Avenue.

"How about the two who left?" Sandro asked.

"Kitty and Lucy," said Ginger. She had his pants open. Sandro stood and slipped them off. Ginger took the pants and carefully folded them over a chair. She rubbed her hands through the hair on Sandro's chest, then put her arms around him. Sandro could feel her breasts, soft warm mounds against him.

"Where did they live?" Sandro pressed.

"Off with those shorts first, come on, the whole thing."

Ginger reached down and closed her hand softly on him. "Oh,

baby, you are ripe and beautiful," she said, pushing him gently back onto the bed.

The room was filled with incense, heavy and warming.

"Kitty lived in Queens," she said, moving toward him, mounting onto the bed with one knee.

"Hold it. Wait a minute," said Sandro, moving her back. "Is she the only one you know about who's lived in Queens?"

"The only one since I've been at the club. That's almost three years."

"Do you know where she lives?" Sandro said.

"I have her address in my book," Ginger replied.

"Get it for me, please."

Ginger looked quizzically at Sandro. She walked to the other side of the bed and took out a small leather-bound book. Sandro twisted onto his stomach and pulled the pink Princess phone toward him. He dialed the number Gianni had given him, which was the regular number of the garage.

"Hello, this is Sandro Luca. Is Gianni there?"

"Just a minute," said Angie the Kid. "How you doin', Mr. Luca? This is Angie the Kid."

"Fine, Angie, fine. Let me speak to Gianni."

"Okay, I'll put him right on."

There was silence, and then the phone was picked up.

"Hello, Sandro, what did you get?"

"I'm not sure of that yet. Wait a second." Sandro looked over at Ginger, holding his hand over the mouthpiece.

"The only thing I've got is Crestwood Village, Wood-side," said Ginger, shrugging.

"Gianni, the only thing I can get is Crestwood Village, Woodside."

"What's her name?"

"Her name is Kitty—" Sandro looked to Ginger.

"Johnson."

"Johnson," repeated Sandro.

"Kitty Johnson, Crestwood Village, Woodside," Gianni said.

"She's the only colored bunny who's lived in Queens in the last two or three years," said Sandro.

"That's great, Sandro. That's really great."

"Okay, Gianni. I'll check with you later." Sandro hung up the phone, as he watched Ginger put the address book away. She hooked her thumbs under the filmy bikini pants, and slid them down her soft thighs. She got onto the bed, lifting herself up on one knee, then the other, until she knelt on the bed close to Sandro. She leaned forward. Sandro reached up, caressing her breasts, one in each hand, supporting her as her weight came forward. He eased her down on top of himself, their mouths fusing as the candle lifted its exotic incense into the room.

3:00 P.M.

Joey and Bobby Matteawan found Crestwood Village, a small housing development just off the Grand Central Parkway in Queens, near La Guardia Air Terminal. There were six brick buildings in the development, each eight stories high, each containing 64 apartments. Joey and Bobby Matteawan went to each building and checked the names next to the bells. There were two Johnsons. One was in the first building they went into: C. JOHNSON. The other was in the fifth building: just JOHNSON. They decided that C. Johnson was not the right party, and headed for the fifth building to try plain Johnson first.

They entered it and stood in the vestibule studying the large, polished chrome bank of apartment bells with names next to them.

"Here's Johnson—3F," said Bobby Matteawan.

"Ring it," said Joey.

Bobby Matteawan rang. They waited. There was no answer. They rang again. Still no answer.

"Try somebody else," said Joey.

Bobby Matteawan pressed the bell next to the name H. Schwarz. They waited.

"Yes?" a woman's voice inquired metallically over the intercom.

"Parcel post," Bobby Matteawan replied.

A buzzer sounded, releasing the lock on the front door. Bobby Matteawan and Joey walked in. They entered the automatic elevator and rose to the third floor; no one was in the hallway. Joey pushed the doorbell of apartment 3F while Bobby Matteawan watched the other end of the hall and the elevator. No one answered the bell. Joey rang again, and once again.

"No one home," Bobby Matteawan said.

"Okay," said Joey, attending to the lock with two small metal picks. Bobby Matteawan shielded him from the view of anyone who might have entered the hallway. With his left hand Joey slipped a small metal rod into the lock, using it as a tension bar. With his right he inserted another small sharp instrument and within seconds his deft touches picked the lock. He twisted the cylinder.

"There it is," he said.

They both moved quickly into the silent dark apartment, closing the door behind them. Matteawan searched the living room carefully, without ransacking it. Joey tackled the bedroom. They were looking for the pictures and ashtrays that Bianco had described. Bobby Matteawan searched a pile of mail on a table near the entry. They met at the bedroom door.

"This doesn't look like it," said Bobby Matteawan.

"That C. Johnson must be Catherine for Kitty," said Joey.

"Shit! Let's try the other place." Bobby Matteawan spied a small gold box on top of a chest against the wall and put it in his pocket.

Suddenly, they heard a key being inserted into the front door. They froze. The door swung open. A woman and a man, both elderly, both with grocery bundles in their arms, entered. The man reached out one finger beyond his bundles to flip on the light switch. Their mouths flopped open, their eyes widened with shock as they saw two men in coats and hats standing in their living room.

"Hey, what are you doing here?" said the startled man.

"Don't worry, folks," Joey said consolingly, "I'm Detective Johnson. This is Detective Radmer. We're from the precinct. We had reports of prowlers over here and we're just checking everything out. Sorry to frighten you."

"You're the police?" the woman gasped, almost hysterical. "You're the police?" She was repeatedly pressing her hand against her chest, as if her breath wouldn't come unless she helped it. Her husband stood numb.

"That's right, ma'am," Joey continued, "we had the superintendent let us into the building. We're just going up the fire escape here, checking out the other apartments in this line. We had a report of some prowlers around this line of the building."

"Oh my God, thank God it's the police!" the woman exclaimed, still pressing her chest.

"Is everything all right, officer?" asked the man.

"Everything is fine," Bobby Matteawan told them.

Joey smiled reassuringly.

"Let's put these packages down, mother," said the man. They both moved toward the kitchen, which was just off the living room.

As the couple entered it, Joey and Bobby Matteawan hurried out the front door. Once in the public hallway, they scampered for the exit door and plunged down the interior stairway, their feet booming on the steps until they reached the bottom. Once in the lobby, they walked calmly to the car. Bobby Matteawan started the engine and the car moved slowly away from the curb, to be lost in traffic on Queens Boulevard.

"Holy Christ!" said Bobby Matteawan, turning to Joey. "How did you think up that one?"

"What was I supposed to say, that we're burglars?"

"Boy, that was great!" said Bobby Matteawan. "Well, at least I got something in that joint besides almost getting pinched." He reached into his pocket and took out the gold box. It was small and not real gold. Bobby Matteawan handed it to Joey, who opened it. Inside it were just some ashes. A white piece of paper was attached to the underside of the lid. It read:

CONTAINED HEREIN ARE THE REMAINS
OF OUR BELOVED DAUGHTER MARJORY
JANUARY 7, 1943–JUNE 15, 1959

Joey read the legend, then slowly shut the box. He looked out the side window quietly.

"What's it say?" asked Bobby Matteawan, watching the traffic ahead.

"That this is all that's left of their daughter. She was only sixteen. Christ."

"*What?*" Bobby Matteawan turned quickly toward Joey.

"Their daughter died when she was sixteen years old. They creemated her."

"Holy shit!" said Bobby Matteawan. "That box's worse than a *malocchia*—throw the goddamn thing out the window."

"No," Joey said firmly. "Take me back there."

"Hey, I'm supposed to be crazy, not you."

"We got to bust the other apartment anyway," said Joey.

"The cops'll be all over the place," Bobby Matteawan protested.

"You'll keep look-out. I'll go in. Take me back," Joey repeated.

Bobby Matteawan saw the determination on Joey's face. Bobby Matteawan knew how determined Joey could be. He made a U-turn and drove back to the house, stopping at the corner. An empty police car stood at the curb, its red light revolving.

"They must be upstairs," said Joey. "You wait here. I'll be right back." He entered the building and pressed a random bell, again announcing himself as parcel post. The buzzer sounded and Joey entered, heading toward the emergency stairway. He put the gold box in a corner, and walked back to the bell panel. He buzzed apartment 3F.

"Who is it?" asked a female voice.

"Your gold box is in the corner of the emergency stairway on the ground floor."

There was silence for a moment. "*What?* Who is it?"

Joey repeated his curt message and walked out of the building and made his way back to the car.

They drove around for about a half hour, then returned to Crestwood Village. There were no police visible now. They went to the first building. "Let's get going," said Joey. "I'll stay down here and keep an eye on things outside. You go ahead in and bust the apartment. If the cops come, I'll get in and ring the bell three times. You come right down."

"Okay," said Bobby Matteawan.

Separately, the two men crossed the walks. Bobby entered the building and rang the bell marked C. JOHNSON, 6F. There was no answer. Using the parcel post dodge on a random bell, Bobby Matteawan entered the building. He went directly to apartment 6F and rang the bell. There was no answer. Quickly he took out his picks, and with lightning speed opened the apartment and disappeared inside. He took off his hat and coat and began his search. He saw several photographs of a colored bunny with some other girls and men. He wanted to be sure. He was searching the bedroom when he heard the bell ring three times. He had to move quickly. This must be the place. He moved toward the wall to grab a picture to take with him. He heard footsteps pounding in the hallway outside. Bobby Matteawan turned in a panic—there was no place to hide. The police pushed open the door, their guns drawn.

A split second before the police entered, Bobby Matteawan switched on the lights and lit a cigarette.

"Okay, hoist them," said one of the cops.

"What? Are you talking to me?" Bobby Matteawan sounded totally surprised.

"Listen, punk," said the other cop, bearing down on Bobby Matteawan with his pistol drawn.

"Are you policemen crazy?" Bobby Matteawan asked incredulously.

"What do you mean, are we crazy?" the first cop said. They looked at each other quickly.

"This is my apartment. What are *you* doing here?" Bobby Matteawan said calmly. He sat on the sofa, flicking his ashes in an ashtray on a side table.

"Your apartment?" the second cop asked.

"Of course it's my apartment. What do you think I'm doing here? Sit down, officers. And please, your guns aren't necessary."

The cops stared at Bobby Matteawan. "We've got a report of a burglary in progress and we find you in the apartment. That's good enough for us."

"I sure appreciate your responding so quickly. Usually you can't find a cop when you need one. But I really live here." Bobby Matteawan rose and walked into the kitchen and opened the refrigerator. "Would you fellows like a beer?"

"What's your name?" the police demanded, unconvinced.

"Johnson. Charles Johnson," Bobby Matteawan replied. "Look at the bell outside." He took out a can of beer and opened it. He took a glass from the sink, and poured the beer into it. He walked back to the living room and sat down.

The cops watched him wordlessly, their drawn pistols beginning to drop.

"I think you fellows are doing a fabulous job. Really terrific. Except that I really do live here. I appreciate your coming over, though."

"Let me see some identification," demanded the second cop.

Bobby Matteawan rose and walked toward the bedroom. "Sure, just a minute and I'll get my wallet."

"Hello, officers," a woman's voice said. Bobby Matteawan was inside the bedroom and couldn't see her, but he could hear her voice. It meant trouble.

"Yes, ma'am? Can we help you?" he heard the cops asking her.

"I live across the hall. I'm the one who called you."

"Madam, come in here please," one of the cops said. His voice was strong and cutting.

"Come on out here, mister," demanded the other cop.

Bobby Matteawan came out, a sheepish smile on his face. The cops' pistols were directly trained on him. He wanted to bull his way out now—to tell Joey this was the right apartment. But the cops were spread apart, ready to grab him.

"Is this the man who lives here, lady?" one of the cops asked the woman.

"*Him*? Of course he doesn't live here. It's a colored girl lives here. A beautiful girl, not a criminal like that."

"You're sure, lady?"

"Of course I'm sure. I've been living here 25 years and I should know who my neighbors are."

The cops looked at Bobby Matteawan, anger flushing their necks and faces.

"Okay lady, that's fine. Thank you," said one cop. "We'll take care of this now." He motioned for her to leave.

"You can go now, lady," said the other cop. "We'll be over to see you when we finish here."

"All right, officer. Thank you very much. You won't let this criminal go?" The woman was frightened.

"Not on a bet, lady," one of the cops assured her.

The cops waited, listening to the woman's fading footsteps. Then they turned toward Bobby Matteawan. The first cop strode across the room and grabbed the front of Bobby Matteawan's shirt. The shirt ripped down the front as he pulled Bobby Matteawan toward him.

"You lousy punk," the cop said, as his fist cracked into the side of Bobby Matteawan's head.

Bobby Matteawan lunged at him.

"Hold it, punk," the second cop warned, his gun trained on Bobby Matteawan's belly.

The first cop stuffed his fist into Bobby Matteawan's stomach. As Bobby Matteawan bent forward, the cop cuffed him on the back of the head.

"Don't overdo it, Frank," the cop with the gun advised. "Let's get him down to the station house."

"I'd like to stuff this punk through the keyhole," said the first cop.

Bobby Matteawan was bleeding from the mouth. "Fuck you, cop," he said.

"When I get you down the station house, punk, I'm going to knock your brains out," the cop said.

"If you tell your buddy with the gun to put it down, I'll kick the shit out of the both of you. I'll stuff that gun—"

Another punch in the stomach kept Bobby Matteawan from talking as the cops led him out of the house.

4:30 P.M.

"Send somebody to bail Bobby out," Gianni said to Frankie the Pig.

"I've taken care of it," Frankie the Pig assured him. "I got our regular bondsman to call one of his friends in Queens. He'll have him bailed out as soon as he's arraigned."

"When will that be?"

"He didn't think it'd be before seven or seven-thirty tonight. They have to go to court to be arraigned and have bail set."

Gianni frowned. He turned to Joey, who was sitting beside the desk in the garage office. Tony was standing in the background. "Then what happened?"

"When they took Bobby Matteawan downstairs, he had the cuffs behind his back," said Joey. "I couldn't stay too close. I was thinking the cops might bring down the people from that first apartment to identify him. And if they saw me, I'd be in the can too."

"You did exactly the right thing," Gianni assured him. "I can't have two men out of action—we need everyone we have. Did he get to say anything, did he get any word to you about whether it was the right apartment or not?"

"I'm not sure," Joey said. "He was making a racket, though. I mean, you don't know Bobby Matteawan too well. But he doesn't like being arrested. It usually takes about six cops to get him to the station house. I was away down the street pretty much but I could hear that one of the things he was screaming was *'yes, yes.'* Now I don't know if he meant the apartment or not; I think so, but I'm just not sure."

Gianni looked at Frankie the Pig. "I don't know either. But I'd guess that we should assume it was."

"Could we get Sandro Luca to go out to the police station and talk to him? Then we wouldn't have to waste too much time if we're wrong."

"That's a good idea, Frankie," said Gianni. "Now all we have to do is track down Luca."

"Did he say where he was when he called?" Frankie asked.

"I know where he was, but I don't know the exact location," Gianni said, knowing Frankie the Pig would neither understand nor approve of Sandro's present occupation. "He said he'd be around this afternoon."

"When he comes, should I send him out to Queens?" asked Frankie the Pig.

"When he comes in, we'll ask him if he'd mind going out there," said Gianni. "One of the boys can drive him."

Frankie the Pig nodded. "What do you want done in the meantime, Gianni?"

"Well, if we assume that this was the chocolate bunny's apartment, we've got to figure out where her friends are—the guys who did the kidnaping. They're apparently not holding Sal in that apartment."

"Why do you say that?" Tony asked.

"They'd never have let Bobby out alive," said Gianni.

"I guess that's right," said Frankie the Pig.

"How do we find her friends?" Tony continued.

"First, we've got to find her. If that's her apartment, she wasn't there either," said Gianni.

"Why not?"

"Because Joey would have seen her. She'd have gone down to the station house with the cops, or right after them in one of the squad cars. So the first thing we have to do is find that girl," said Gianni. "We know she doesn't work in the Playboy Club any more."

"Sandro tell you that?" asked Frankie the Pig.

Gianni nodded. "I think Big Diamond might be able to help us on this. He knows the colored parts of the Bronx and Manhattan like the back of his hand. Maybe he'd know where this girl operates."

"You want me to call him?"

"Yes. Ask him if he knows something about a girl who used to be a Playboy bunny. Maybe she's working in some other place he knows about. Those girls usually stay in the same line—they get too used to the fast, easy tips and the action."

Frankie the Pig went to the wall phone.

"On second thought, let Tony speak to Big Diamond," Gianni said. "No sense confusing him with too many new people. Big Diamond knows Tony already."

Frankie the Pig shrugged.

"I hope the cops don't figure out who Bobby Matteawan is," said Frankie the Pig, looking at Gianni.

"What do you mean?"

"Well, you said there's a tap on the restaurant phone line we've got here. That means the cops know what's going on. If the cops in Queens figure out that he's with us, and they let the cops here know about it, they might rough him up trying to get the information they couldn't get out of you this morning."

"That's a very real possibility," Gianni said.

"Big Diamond says he'll come down," said Tony, holding his hand over the mouthpiece. "He says he wants to see his man, Gianni."

Gianni smiled. "Tell him I don't want to put him to all that trouble."

"He insists on coming." Tony said a few more words, then hung up.

Gianni turned back to Frankie: "Will Bobby stand up?"

"Bobby Matteawan?" said Frankie the Pig. "They'd have to hit him in the head with an ax, and he still wouldn't give them the sweat off his balls."

"Well then, we don't have to worry about that," said Gianni.

Sandro entered the garage, carrying his briefcase. He looked as shiny and fresh as when Gianni had seen him early that morning.

"Hello, Sandro." Gianni smiled at him.

Sandro's eyes returned the smile. "I found out something else," he said.

"I hope you didn't have to sweat this information out of your informant," said Gianni.

Sandro reddened. "I found out that your ex-bunny works in a bar uptown called the Pirate's Den. She's a barmaid or a waitress there."

"Where is it?" asked Frankie the Pig.

"On Amsterdam Avenue near 140th Street—somewhere around there."

"That's great, Sandro," said Gianni.

"Should we send somebody up there to get this dame?" asked Frankie the Pig.

"Not yet," said Gianni. "Big Diamond said he was coming down. We'll let him figure out how to move on this Pirate's Den."

"That's a good idea," said Frankie the Pig.

"Meanwhile, Sandro, one of our boys has been arrested out at Crestwood Village while he was trying to find this Johnson girl's apartment. We don't know if he found it or not. So, I'd be very grateful if you'd go to the precinct and talk to Bobby—ask him if that was the right place. Gus'll drive you."

Sandro studied Gianni. "If it didn't have to do with this case, I sure as hell wouldn't. But how can I turn you down?"

"Thank you, Sandro," said Gianni.

"I'd better get out there before they take him to court."

"If you manage to talk to him, call me here," said Gianni.

"Right." Sandro left with Gus trailing behind him.

Gianni lit a cigarette and looked at his watch. It was only 5: 15—still almost three hours until they would receive the next phone call.

"We've got to make sure that Sal's still alive," Gianni said to no one in particular.

"Those bastards," said Frankie the Pig. "Those miserable niggers."

Just then the door of the garage opened as Big Diamond bent low and entered. He stood tall, a fat cigar in his mouth, his beige fedora at a rakish tilt. He was dressed in a brown suit with a beige shirt and beige silk tie. His shoes were golden brown, and shined to sparkling. Lloyd came in behind Big Diamond. He stood, dark and stern, next to Big Diamond, looking around apprehensively.

"Did I hear someone complaining about my people, or talking about those worthless niggers who took your friend, Gianni?" he said, a big smile on his face.

"Ah, you big son of a bitch," said Gianni. The two men embraced, clapping each other on the back.

"Son of a bitch yourself," said Big Diamond. "You getting stronger and handsomer than ever. Lloyd—" he turned, "Gianni, this here is Lloyd, my main man. Lloyd, this is Gianni, the Silver Eagle. Man, he used to turn those silver curls on the broads and they'd be out cold—I mean done, signed, sealed and delivered." Big Diamond gave out with a big laugh and put his arm around Gianni's shoulders.

"And what about you?" said Gianni. "He'd get these little dames, pick them up in the air and dance them all over the floor without their feet touching the ground. They'd feel his muscles and they'd be done for."

They both laughed again.

"Come on into my fancy office," said Gianni.

"It's no worse than some of the places we have to work out of sometimes—right, Lloyd?" said Big Diamond. "Matter of fact, it's better than some." He settled back in a chair. "Well now, any news on Sal?"

"Not yet. We expect a call about eight o'clock," said Gianni. "Did you pick up any news for us?"

"Nothing much," replied Big Diamond. "Lloyd's been going around, and so have the rest of our guys, but we can't raise too much noise. We don't want these people to go underground."

"Well, we've got a possible lead in your area," said Gianni. "One of the men involved in this may be going with a girl named Kitty Johnson, who lives in Queens—and I think she's a barmaid in a joint called the Pirate's Den."

"That's what it is exactly," said Big Diamond, "a joint."

Lloyd nodded agreement. "A lot of small-time chiselers, punks and junkies hang out there. You picked the right place, all right."

"Can we get some information on this girl and her boyfriend?"

"Oh, we'll get it all right, Gianni," said Big Diamond. "We'll go right back now, and I'll send over a couple of guys who won't raise too much notice. What do you want to know?"

"I want to know if she's got some special guy; if she's in tight with any group we might check out on this kidnaping."

"Can you do that, Lloyd?" Big Diamond asked.

"Sure, Big," replied Lloyd. "You want it, we'll do it. I'll send a couple of guys in there. You want me to call them now?"

"No, we'll go back. I think we should pick them personally. If we screw it up, there's one of our friends going to be killed."

"I appreciate it," said Gianni.

"Now don't give me that appreciation shit. You're my man—I owe it to you, you owe it to me. We do it because we're old-timers from old times. Right, Gianni?"

"You're right, Big," Gianni smiled. "A hundred percent. It's nice to know there are still a few of us who feel that way."

"It's sweet to be able to do it, Gianni. It really is. Oh, yes," he said, turning to Lloyd and putting out his hand. Lloyd handed him an envelope. Big Diamond handed it to Gianni.

"What's this?" asked Gianni.

"It's some long green," Big Diamond said, "in case you need a little extra. There's ten large there."

"No, no," Gianni said. "I can't take this."

"You bet your ass you can. If you don't need it, you give it back. But if you need it, I want you to use it." He pressed the envelope in Gianni's hand. "I'm not doing this for you, I'm doing it for me. 'Cause when I get snatched, I want to know my boys have someplace to come and put the touch." Big Diamond laughed.

The phone rang. Tony picked it up. "It's for you, Gianni."

It was Sandro. "Wait a minute, Big," Gianni said. "I may have something else."

Big Diamond and Lloyd stood by the door, watching Gianni on the phone. He hung up and looked at them. "One of our boys got arrested in this Kitty Johnson's apartment. The lawyer just spoke to him," said Gianni. "She's the right girl all right. Now when we find out who her friends are, we're going to be breathing on their necks."

"Man, if anybody can breathe hot on their necks, it's me and Lloyd: right, Lloyd?"

Lloyd nodded, his face stern, his lips drawn tight. "We'll find them."

Tony, who was watching from the doorway, liked Lloyd, he liked the way he worked. "You need any help breathing, just give me a ring: I breathe pretty good too," said Tony.

"I'll find them, and you take it from there," said Lloyd.

"That's a deal," said Tony.

"Come on, now, let's go," said Big Diamond. "We'll call you as soon as we get the information."

"As fast as you can, Big," said Gianni.

"Even faster than that," said Big Diamond, waving as he and Lloyd walked out of the garage.

7:50 P.M.

"Fifty-five, sixty. Sixty thousand here," said Frankie the Pig, counting packages of hundred dollar bills in five-thousand-dollar wrappers. The packages were piled on the office desk. Gianni watched him count. Tony and Gus were standing by the door. Outside in the garage Angie the Kid and Bobby Matteawan were sitting on a bench, watching TV.

"And here's the other ten from Big Diamond," said Gianni, handing over the envelope.

"That makes seventy," said Frankie the Pig.

"That big nigger's all right," allowed Tony.

"He sure is," said Gianni, taking an envelope from his inside jacket pocket. "Here's twenty-five more."

Frankie the Pig looked at Gianni as he took the envelope from him, adding it to the pile on the table. "Now we have what we need."

"We have to have it all," said Gianni. "But I'll try to bargain them down."

"Will we pay them tonight?" Tony asked.

"I'm going to try to stall them. See if we can get another day out of it," said Gianni, "now that we're making some progress."

"Right," said Tony; "if we can track down this dame, we can track down her boyfriend."

Bobby Matteawan came in the door. "Yeah, we'll get his name out of her." A satanic look of pleasure gleamed in his eyes.

"And when we get the boyfriend, we'll get them all," said Frankie the Pig. "They'll be sorry they were ever born on this earth."

"Come on," said Gianni, calling them back to the matter at hand. "I'm more interested in getting Sal back alive than in tortures and killing."

The others looked at him.

"That's right," Gianni repeated firmly, looking at them each in turn. "I want Sal. I want them, too, but I'm not licking my chops over their blood." Gianni fell silent, drawing back from what had been gnawing at him for two days.

"I'll take your share, Gianni," said Bobby Matteawan.

"I'm not in this for blood," Gianni repeated. "I'm in it for Sal."

"So are we, so are we," said Frankie the Pig. "But these bastards and all their friends have to be taught a lesson they won't ever forget. How are you going to handle them once we get hold of them, Gianni?"

"I'm not worrying about that yet," Gianni said carefully. "After I get Sal back, I'll see. Right now, I've got more important things on my mind. Or don't you agree?"

They looked sheepish, wilting before Gianni's strength.

"We better be sure we do get Sal back," said Frankie the Pig.

"And get him alive," added Gianni.

The thought brought them up short.

"You think they'd kill Sal?" asked Gus.

"The slimy bastards," said Tony.

"We have to include that possibility," said Gianni.

"How can we guarantee we get him back alive?" asked Frankie the Pig.

"I'm not sure yet," said Gianni. "That's something I have to work out with them tonight. I'm not buying a cat in a bag, even if the cat is Sal."

The phone rang, its sound taking the breath out of them. Gianni's hand reached out for it automatically.

"No, it's the wall phone," said Tony, pointing to it. He picked up the receiver. "It's for you, Gianni. It's Big Diamond."

Gianni rose swiftly and took it.

"Gianni, this is Big. We got that girl. She was working behind the bar."

"Does she know anything?" asked Gianni.

"Don't know yet. We took her right out of the place. Lloyd and a couple of his guys are taking her to an apartment they've got. They're going to talk to her."

"You want me to send someone up there?" Gianni said.

"No, thanks—we can handle a girl. Christ, Gianni. What kind of boys you think I have anyway?" Big Diamond started to laugh. "You guys just sit tight, we'll get some information for you in a little. I'll call you back. I just wanted you to know we're moving right along."

"All right. I'll be here. All night if necessary."

Gianni hung up just as the other phone was beginning to ring. He picked up the receiver, realizing as he did so that Sal's life was on the line. He also realized that the police were on the line too.

"Hello Mister Big," said the same deep voice from the night before. "You guys ready to do some business?"

"We're ready."

Feigin and Schmidt at the listening post had their earphones on. They winked at each other. The tape machine was recording.

"Good. Now, you got the bread, man?"

"Not a hundred," said Gianni.

"What you mean, not a hundred?" asked the voice. "I told you a hundred, and that's what we want."

"It's not easy to raise that much so fast," said Gianni calmly. "We've got seventy."

"Seventy? You kidding me, man? I should have told you a hundred fifty, then you'd come up with the hundred. You better get that other thirty real fast, or you're going to get a real dead man real fast."

"Don't go getting steamed," said Gianni softly. "Seventy isn't chicken feed either. We don't make funny money and it's tough to come by a lot of cash these days."

"You can get it," said the voice.

"We scraped everywhere we could, believe me. We don't have a bank we can go to. Seventy is all we could get. What the hell. Seventy goes a long way. It buys a lot of living," Gianni said.

"Not long enough, man. We got a lot to make up for."

"What will killing the old man do for you? Give you a five-second charge? That charge won't buy a thing," said Gianni.

"Seventy's not enough," the voice insisted.

"I can't get a hundred," said Gianni.

"You damn well better."

"How do I know the old man is still alive? I don't want to buy a recording."

The voice laughed. "You guys won't get a recording. I know who I'm dealing with."

"How do we know that? I mean, if I can scrape a couple more bucks together, how do I know I still have a live man?"

"You think I'd lie to you, man? If I say you'll get your man, you'll get him. How much more you going to get?"

"Maybe another five thousand," said Gianni.

"Hey, man, don't fuck with me," said the voice, hostile and vicious suddenly. "You think you fucking around with some shit heel?"

"Don't get hot under the collar," Gianni said coolly. "We don't just reach into the air and pick out five thousand—just think of it, if you had to come up with five thousand in three seconds, where would you turn? Same with us. We got to scrape it up."

"Don't bullshit me, man. You got to do better than that," said the voice.

"I can't come up with it right now—I mean I'll need some time."

"Hey, man, I think you think we're fucking around. Remember that guy we threw out the car the other night? Man, your friend is an old man, he's lighter than the other guy. We'll throw him right through the window into your lap, you fuck with us."

"I'm not. I'm trying to make a legitimate deal with you—straight, on the level. You've got us over a barrel, and I'm playing your game. I'm telling you straight: I'll try to get more money. But I need some time on it."

The others in the room were listening intently. Bobby Matteawan was outside in the garage, pacing, excited and nervous.

Schmidt and Feigin were looking at each other, their faces reacting as the conversation unfolded.

"That's right, we got you over a barrel, and we going to keep you there from now on. You ain't going to be able to string this thing out and keep playing games with us, man," said the voice.

"I'm not trying to. I know when someone means business," said Gianni, "and I know when I'm in a tight spot. This is one of them—I'd be crazy to try to string it out."

"That's the truth."

"I just need time to get some extra money. As it is, we've tapped everybody we know and we're still short of a hundred. But I figure we can get more. I don't know where, but I'm going to get it."

"That's your problem," said the voice.

"But how will I know I'm buying a real live body, and not a stiff?" Gianni asked. "That's just as important."

"You get the money, ready to move, and I'll let you talk to the old man. That good enough?"

"It's good for openers," said Gianni.

"Openers? Don't try to get cute with me, man, or I'll cut this man's throat myself."

"Cut his throat and you'll end up with nothing. Why kill him? I'm willing to come up with the money. You get the money, give me the old man. Killing him won't even buy you a tie."

"How much you going to get up?" asked the voice.

"Eighty thousand."

"It's got to be ninety," said the voice.

"Give me one more day and I'll get eighty-five. Not a penny more. I can't get it up. Eighty-five tomorrow night."

"You can't string it out past this time tomorrow. If I call tomorrow and you start talking trash again, your man is dead."

"I'll get it," said Gianni.

"He'll be right here. I'll let you listen while I cut his throat, you start talking trash tomorrow," warned the voice.

Gianni was wondering if the cops were listening to all of this and what they might try to do about it. He hoped they wouldn't mess things up by trying to help.

"You won't have to cut his throat. I'll get it. Eighty-five, agreed?"

"Cash. We'll count it first. You try and fuck us with some funny stuff, and we cut his throat anyway."

"Wait a minute. I get him back when you get the money. Same time—it's a trade," said Gianni.

"Bullshit, man. You think we're crazy? We get the money first, then you get your man."

"How can I know that?" asked Gianni, concerned now.

"You got to trust us," said the voice.

"Now don't you fuck with me," said Gianni, his voice hardening. "I'm not buying any cat in a bag."

"You going to do it my way, man. This is my show."

"We'll have to agree on something," said Gianni. "My mother didn't raise any idiot children."

"You tell me what you have in mind, I'll tell you if I agree," said the voice.

"Where's the payoff going to be?" asked Gianni.

"Hey, man, my momma didn't raise no idiots either. You think I'm going to tell you that now so you can go get it rigged?"

"When will I know?" said Gianni.

"You be at the phone tomorrow night, with the bread, and you'll get the instructions. You go where we tell you and you'll get another call there. Then you'll be told where to make the payoff."

"But there's got to be an exchange. No exchange, no money," said Gianni.

"Hey, man, you're not in the driver's seat, we are."

"You're not dealing with children," said Gianni. "We've been through tough scrapes before; so's that old man you got with you. We don't scare easy either. You want to make a deal, we'll make the deal. Nobody's going to fuck us around though."

"Ain't nobody's fucking us around either," said the voice.

"Nobody's trying to."

"I'll call tomorrow night," said the voice.

"I'll be ready."

"It's business or else, tomorrow night. Eight o'clock."

"Business it'll be, on both sides," said Gianni.

"I'll think about that," said the voice.

"No thinking about it. We came through on our end, you come through on yours. We want some assurance we're getting a live man back—we don't want a body. You bury the body. It isn't worth eighty-five thousand to us just to bury it."

"Tomorrow night, eight o'clock," said the voice. The phone went dead against Gianni's ear.

8:30 P.M.

"We going to off this old man or they going to pay?" asked Alfred intently, his eyes staring into Bull's.

"They'll pay," Bull assured him.

"What's this shit about tomorrow night?" Yank asked. He was leaning against the table next to Hartley, who was pouring a drink for himself.

"Yeah, man, what the hell you tell him it was okay for tomorrow?" asked Hartley. "You know it's getting hot around town. There are colored cats looking for us now."

"Because they didn't have enough money," answered Bull flatly. "I don't mind pushing them out of our place, man. But that bread is important too. It's what we need to set up our own operations, our own banks."

"Man, we got a hundred-fifteen thousand already," said Hartley, "and it's plenty, man, plenty. You know how much that is, five ways?

Why didn't you tell the cat we'd take it and get rid of this shit tonight? The longer we in, the tougher it is."

"Because two hundred thousand is a nice round figure," said Bull. "Don't we have to set up operations so we can keep in business, keep Harlem for ourselves? Isn't that what we're in this for?"

"Yeah, man," said Duck, sitting on the couch. "Forty thousand dollars, man, forty thousand dollars," he exclaimed jubilantly. "Man, I'm going to get me some threads that'll sing when I walk down the street."

"And man, I'm going to get me a Coupe de Ville, with a heater, and a stereo tape, man, and all that shit they got in them," said Yank.

"Listen, you two jerk-offs," said Bull abruptly. "I thought I made it clear, ain't nobody going to spend nothing for three or four months." He looked at the others. "And ain't nobody getting all his bread. Half goes into a kitty for operations."

"Man, we ain't spending, we just dreaming," apologized Duck.

"Dreaming like that leads to trouble," said Bull. "Just forget even dreaming about that money for three, four months."

"How come you let that guinea white fuck take you for fifteen thousand?" Alfred asked. "You should have told him to fuck himself. Man, I'd kill that old man for fifteen thousand as soon as I'd walk across the street."

"He didn't take me for fifteen thousand, man, we took him for eighty-five. You do your thinking with the wrong end of your body," said Bull.

"Yeah, man, that's the way to look at it," said Yank. "What the hell's the difference—eighty-five, a hundred." He poured himself a drink. "I think we ought to have a drink for luck."

"Tomorrow, while we're counting the money," said Bull.

"You know, I'm just a little worried about these nigger cats prowling around looking for someone," said Hartley.

"Let them look—black cats, white cats, don't make no difference. We all still working, normal, just like everyday slaves for the white-master racket guys. We keep working, they keep getting their money, and they keep looking for someone else."

"But you heard what's traveling around—Big Diamond is on the prowl. And that Lloyd ain't no shitass."

"Yes he is," said Alfred. "And I'll cut his ass from one side to the other, that Uncle Tom shit, kissing the ass of that other big motherfucking Tom, Big Diamond. It's time all the shit gets thrown out of our places, nigger and whitey both."

"Right on," said Duck. "Them Uncle Toms is next. We ain't working for them neither. They work for whitey, they want to be whitey, well, let them float in the river right next to whitey."

"Yeah, yeah, but not now, man," said Bull. "We got to think of a payoff where we ain't going to be caught with our asses sticking out. We got to figure how to arrange the payoff."

"You can do it, Bull. You done all the others," said Hartley.

"All the other payoffs been in New York or the Bronx," said Bull. "Maybe we make this one in Queens. That's it, man, in Queens. There's lots of good places there, and nobody'd think of that. Who the fuck ever thinks of Queens?"

"Cool," said Duck.

"When you want us to get the old man and bring him in?" asked Yank.

"Not until tomorrow."

"That was cool, man," said Hartley. "Hiding this one in Newark. Who the hell would think he was there?"

"Good thing we got girlfriends all over the place," Bull smiled. "This way they can't find any pattern to follow."

"Right on," said Hartley, raising his glass in salute.

"Why don't we all get in your car, Yank. Let's take a ride to Queens. We'll find some big open place where they ain't going to trap us. Ain't no whitey going to trap this here boy."

THURSDAY, FEBRUARY 11

9:30 A.M.

LIEUTENANT SCHMIDT SAT BEHIND HIS DESK, blowing smoke ceiling-ward. Feigin was pouring a cup of coffee.

"We sure don't have much to work on," said Feigin.

"We sure don't."

Quinn entered the office and went directly to the coffee pot. "I got Communications," he said to the lieutenant.

"And?"

"They'll have men standing by in each of the five boroughs. As soon as the colored guy gives Gianni the place to go to for the additional information, Communications will work fast and wire the place by the time Gianni's people get there."

"Then what?" asked Feigin.

"Then we'll have to move fast," said Schmidt. "Did you tell Communications that I want a man on each wire? Once we get the location, we can move men directly to the payoff."

"I told them," said Quinn.

"Meanwhile, we drive to the first destination, trying to follow Gianni's boys there ourselves," said Schmidt. "I'm not sure we'll be able to get too close to the payoff scene. That's why we need Communications listening. Other cars can follow by radio. Unless I miss my guess, everything is going to be as much in the open as possible. Those colored guys aren't going to take a chance being trapped."

"And if Aquilino knows we're tapping the phone, he'll try to ditch us anyway," added Feigin.

"I'd bet my shield he knows," said Schmidt. "And I'm sure he'll try to give us the slip. In a way he's right—if the kidnapers see cops, they'll probably kill Sal."

"Actually kill him? I mean, this isn't just some Bowery bum," said Quinn, "or some little pusher from uptown."

Schmidt shrugged. "What the hell do they have to lose? We're not dealing with the same kind of people. The colored guys haven't got anything to begin with. What can happen to them? They'll get killed? The way they probably figure it, so what?

"Either of you got a private car here?"

"I do," said Quinn.

"Good. I've got mine, too," said Schmidt. "We better use those. Sal's boys will recognize even unmarked police cars in a minute. We'll take walkie-talkies so we can keep in touch with headquarters and each other. Did Intelligence come up with anything on this?"

"All we know is that there've been two kidnapings," said Feigin. "One guy is dead. The other guy, who's called Mickey something, we picked up. I think there may have been another, but that's just talk in the street."

"And the one you picked up knew nothing, right?" said Schmidt.

"That's right, Lou," said Feigin. "He's from the Bronx and according to him he wasn't even kidnaped. He didn't know what we were talking about."

"I wonder if Aquilino has anything more than we do?" said Schmidt.

Feigin shrugged as he sipped his coffee.

"You guys better take off, get on the cots upstairs and get some shut-eye. You've been up all night, and we'll probably be up again tonight."

"Say, what the hell kind of job is this anyway?" said Quinn. "Here we are staying up all night, two nights in a row, on a case where there isn't even a case, and the victim doesn't want us to help."

"That just makes it more exciting," Schmidt said, deadpan.

"After twenty years of excitement, it's not so exciting," Quinn grumbled.

"Get some sleep," said Schmidt, picking up a file from his desk. "Ask Ryan to come in here for a minute, will you? I've got other cases to worry about."

10:00 A.M.

Bobby Matteawan was pacing up and down the garage. Angie the Kid was staring at a movie on TV. Tony, Joey, Frankie the Pig and Gus were in the office. They were fidgeting in their chairs, speaking only occasionally. The air seemed charged with electricity.

"Where did you say Gianni went?" asked Frankie the Pig.

"He went up to the Bronx, then out to Brooklyn," said Tony. "He said he had to see some people."

"What for?" asked Frankie the Pig.

"How the hell should I know? He didn't tell me," Tony said curtly.

"Okay, forget it."

"Maybe he went to get some more money?" said Gus.

"What for?" asked Frankie the Pig. "We've got all we need now."

"Hey, don't jump down my throat."

"I think we're all a little jumpy," said Joey.

"Who'd Gianni go with?" asked Frankie the Pig.

"Nobody," replied Tony. "I told him he shouldn't go by himself, that maybe he'd get snatched too. But he made some calls and said nobody'd recognize him anyway."

The garage door opened and a dark colored man entered. Bobby Matteawan stopped his pacing. Angie the Kid stood up, reaching for a tire iron on a work bench. Inside the office, Tony had noticed the action in the outer area. A gun was already in his hand. Frankie the Pig leaped to his feet as he saw the gun being pulled. He saw Tony looking out into the garage and turned, pulling out a pistol of his own.

Another colored man entered. It was Lloyd. He looked around and saw everyone ready for action.

"Okay, okay, this guy's with me," he said.

"I thought it was those creeps that got Sal coming over here for some action," said Bobby Matteawan, starting to pace again.

Angie the Kid sat down, the adrenalin slowly draining back.

"Hello, Lloyd," said Frankie the Pig, coming out of the office. "What's up?"

"We've been moving around all night. I finally found that broad."

"I thought you had her," said Tony.

"Wrong girl," said Lloyd; "she was the new barmaid. Your girl doesn't work there anymore." The fellow who had come in with him was silently looking around at them all. "We had to search through every joint in Harlem till we located her working in another creep joint, the Black Pussy Cafe."

"That sounds like the first place you should have looked," said Tony.

"What'd you do with her?" asked Gus.

"Big said she wouldn't do us any good—it was her friends we wanted," replied Lloyd.

"Did you stake her out?" asked Frankie the Pig.

"Better than that," said Lloyd. "Big had us grab her right out of the bar, just like the first girl."

"How'd you go about it?" asked Gus.

"I just told her somebody wanted to talk to her in one of the booths. I told her it was real important, you know. So when she gets over to the booth, Simon here has a gun inside his coat."

"I had it so only she could see it," said Simon. His voice was deep and resonant.

"Then we got her outside into the car and took her to a place we have. Big was there waiting for us. He started asking her questions."

"She know anything?" asked Tony.

"Not much," said Lloyd.

"Maybe she was bullshitting you," Tony said.

"Man, I didn't conduct a Sunday school lesson," Lloyd said quickly. "That female act don't cut ice with me. And we got what we wanted, all right."

"What?" asked Frankie the Pig. "Come on, for Christ's sake."

"She's got a boyfriend. A guy named Alfred. He's a small-time junk pusher who's sort of attached to another pusher up in Harlem, you know?"

"He's the guy we're looking for?" asked Tony, restive now.

"We're not sure yet," said Lloyd.

"What the hell you mean, you're not sure?" said Tony. "Didn't you get it out of her?"

"She was out of town, down in the Virgin Islands for a few days," Lloyd replied. "Just when this kidnaped guy Mickey was being held in the apartment with the Playboy pictures. She said it sounded like her apartment, all right. But she wasn't there then."

"Are you sure she wasn't bullshitting you?" said Tony.

"Man," said Lloyd slowly, "I told you that the dame wasn't bullshitting. She had a knife right next to her pretty face, and she knew, man, she knew, that thing was going to cut my name into her cheek. She was telling the truth when I finished with her."

"Well, what else did she know?" asked Frankie the Pig.

"She only knows that this guy Alfred has her key and he might have used the apartment."

"Anybody else have a key?"

"She said no," answered Lloyd.

"Where's this Alfred now?"

"Wait a minute. There's more," said Lloyd. "A couple of days after she went down there, Alfred showed up to spend a couple of days fishing. She says that's his thing—fishing for big fish, you know? And she said he had money on him, real money. He was spending it like some fool. She said he rented a captain and boat for two days to take them fishing but they only went for about an hour one day. The rest of the time he was higher than a kite."

"That sounds like our guy," said Gus.

"Did she know about the kidnaping?" asked Frankie the Pig.

"No. She said Alfred told her they got the money from some whitey in New York who spent a couple of days with them. She didn't know what the hell he meant."

"Yeah, but I do," said Tony.

"So do I. Where's this guy Alfred?" asked Frankie the Pig.

"Did you grab him?" asked Tony.

"No. Big said to come down here and talk to Gianni, tell him what went down. Big said it was Gianni's game," replied Lloyd.

"Dammit, don't you at least know where Alfred is?" shouted Frankie the Pig.

"Yeah," Lloyd replied. "A couple of our guys went out to look for him. And they found him."

"Didn't you grab him?"

"No, I told you—Big wouldn't do anything without letting Gianni know what was happening. But we got a guy keeping an eye on him so he don't fly the coop."

"What about the dame? Maybe she'll go back and tell him you were interested in him," said Gus.

"We figured the same thing, so we kept her around. Big said to keep her there until this thing was all over."

"That's good," Tony said.

"Yeah, real good," Frankie the Pig muttered.

"Where's Gianni?" asked Lloyd.

"He's not here. He went out late last night, and hasn't been back since. He's busy," replied Frankie the Pig.

"He's probably going to go right to that hearing he's got today," said Gus.

"That's right, he won't be back for quite a while," said Frankie the Pig. He turned to Lloyd. "Where do we get our hands on this Alfred?"

"You want him *now*?" asked Lloyd.

"Time's getting short. We got to move," said Frankie the Pig.

"Maybe we better wait for Gianni," said Gus.

"What am I, popcorn?" demanded Frankie the Pig. "I'm here, and time is running out—tonight's the payoff. And I say we get this guy and find out where Sal is before it's too late. We'll get it out of him, don't worry."

"Yeah, but maybe Gianni—" Gus said.

"I said we go," Frankie the Pig said with cold authority. "Gianni's not here, and we've got our man sitting like a pigeon. Lloyd, you lead us in your car. We'll follow you."

"I don't think you need so many people," said Lloyd. "It's only one guy and we got him staked out. And if there are too many whites up there, it'll look funny. Besides, we got our own men to handle it."

"I'll go with them," suggested Tony. "This way you'll be here to follow up."

"Okay," said Frankie the Pig, "but don't fuck it up. We need this guy, and we need him right away."

Tony just looked at Frankie the Pig with his cold eyes, his thin lips pressed together. "I won't fuck anything up."

11:30 A.M.

Gianni and Sandro walked down the short stairway of the Criminal Courts building, across the small plaza to Centre Street.

"It's quick work, all right," said Gianni. "They bring in the committee chairman to tell the judge I was given immunity this morning and refused to testify, and then the D.A. makes an application for an order from the judge, and the next thing, I'm in jail if I don't testify. How come the committee's willing to give me immunity?"

"Because they probably know you're not involved in anything," said Sandro, "so they'd rather have your testimony."

"Isn't this a son of a bitch," said Gianni. "They can't put me in jail for something, so they want to put me in jail for nothing."

"And it usually works, Gianni," said Sandro. "They're convinced certain people are no good: you're one of them, and any way they can get you off the street is perfectly fine. I hope you've had some time to think about my suggestion."

"Had some time—look at me, what do I look like this morning?" asked Gianni.

"You look tired, as if you've been up all night."

"I have, first on this business of Sal's, and then I went to a round-table meeting starting about three o'clock this morning. I asked all the big guys to get together," said Gianni. "I told them what I wanted to do about testifying. You know I couldn't just go and do this on my own. First, out of respect. Second, they might not understand. I had to explain it to them."

"And? What happened?" asked Sandro.

"They didn't go for it at first: they said I was taking a chance, and I'd get in difficulty. I explained to them, it was the only way to stop playing right into the cops' hands."

"And?"

"They thought it might work, but they were skeptical. That's when I put in the clincher. I told them I was the perfect guy to do it, because I wasn't involved in anything, so they'd have a tough time pinning anything on me."

"Were they convinced?"

"Convinced is too strong a word, Sandro," said Gianni. They had reached the building where the hearing was being held. The newsmen started to descend upon them again. "They thought it was worth a shot," Gianni continued, "but they weren't interested in taking it themselves."

"How did it end up?" asked Sandro as they walked up the steps. The cameramen were closing in. "Not now, please," said Sandro, stepping in front of Gianni.

"Come on, counselor, not again," said one of the photographers.

"As soon as it's over," said Sandro. "That's what I said the other day, and you got your pictures, didn't you?"

The photographers moved off reluctantly. One of them snapped a picture quickly as he moved away.

"You know, you feel like smacking a sneaky bastard like that in the mouth just because he's a sneak," said Gianni calmly. "I hate sneaks."

"So how did it end up, Gianni?" Sandro repeated. They reached the far end of the anteroom and sat down against the wall.

"It was left that if I wanted to chance it, it was up to me. If I got trapped, it was my own fault."

"Were they worried about your getting them in trouble, testifying about them?" asked Sandro.

Gianni just looked at Sandro blankly, coldly. "Sandro, before anybody goes down because of my tongue—anybody—even if I didn't know him, I'd cut the tongue out. That's the way it is. You know that. You've got the same blood we have. These people are my friends. They'll have to put me in jail for a thousand years before I put a friend in trouble."

Sandro saw Senator Stern walking through the throng. The senator smiled sardonically.

"Hello, Mr. Luca. How are you today?" asked Stern. "I see you have Mr. Aquilino with you."

"Yes. How are you, Senator?"

"I'm fine. Is your man going to testify today?"

"Yes."

Stern's eyes lit up with surprise. "He is?"

"Yes."

Stern nodded thoughtfully, smiling as he turned away.

Sandro turned to Gianni, who was lighting a cigarette. He seemed tired and nervous.

It was not long before the doors of the hearing room closed, and the reporters started to file inside. One of the committee assistants came out and called Gianni's name.

"Well, I guess this is it, Sandro," said Gianni as he rose. "I hope you're right."

Sandro hoped so too. "Just tell the truth," he cautioned. They walked together toward the hearing room. As they reached the door, one of the reporters came over to Gianni.

"I understand you're going to testify today, Mr. Aquilino."

"Whatever happens, you'll hear about it in a couple of minutes," said Sandro.

Stern must already have been at work, Sandro thought, drumming up interest among the reporters.

Sandro and Gianni walked to the witness table. Five members of the committee sat behind a long table. Stern, in the center of the five, asked Gianni to rise and be sworn as a witness.

"Now Mr. Witness," Stern began, "what is your name?"

"Gianni Aquilino."

"And your address, please."

"Chickapea Road, Pawling, New York."

"Are you employed, sir?"

"Yes, I have my own business. Eagle Enterprises."

"And where is that located, sir?"

"475 Fifth Avenue."

"What sort of business is that, Mr. Aquilino?"

"Real estate, commercial investments."

Stern was excited and impatient. "How long have you been engaged in this business, Mr. Aquilino?"

"About 12 years."

"And before that, what business were you engaged in?"

"I was in real estate even then. I was a real estate salesman with Margo Realty in New York."

Next to Gianni, Sandro listened intently, ready to come to his aid if it was necessary. His mind was registering the import of the questions. Safe, so far.

Gianni was unperturbed now that he was on the firing line. He watched Stern calmly, coolly.

"Now, Mr. Aquilino, was there, just before you opened this Eagle Enterprises, on April 15, 1959, an attempt made on your life in the lobby of your apartment building?"

The reporters in the room perked up now. They were listening and watching intently.

"Somebody tried to hold me up in the lobby of my building, as far as I know. And I was shot, yes." Gianni's mind floated back momentarily. Instinctively his hand felt along the ridges of scar tissue on his right temple.

"Now, Mr. Aquilino"—Senator Stern's voice brought him back to the present—"isn't it a fact that you were marked for execution by certain people in the Mafia or Cosa Nostra?"

The other members behind the committee table watched eagerly.

"Let me ask you a question before I answer, Mr. Stern," Gianni said. "What is this Mafia or Cosa Nostra to which you refer?"

Stern's eyes narrowed. "You're asking *me* what the Mafia is?"

"You used the word, Mr. Stern. I can't answer you unless I understand what you're talking about."

"Certainly you know what the Mafia is, Mr. Aquilino." Stern looked up momentarily to see if the reporters were on top of this exchange. They were; their pencils raced across their pads.

"All I know about it is what I read in the newspapers," replied Gianni. "But I'm sure that you have more scientific information with which you could define this Mafia or Cosa Nostra so that I could answer you."

"In 1957, Mr. Aquilino, were you at a meeting of the Mafia in Apalachin?" Stern pressed.

"In 1957 I was arrested in Apalachin as I was on the road, driving home with two friends of mine. I was at no meeting of any organization that I know of."

"Are you saying that you weren't at the Apalachin meeting?"

"What Apalachin meeting, Mr. Stern?" Gianni asked.

Stern's color was deepening. "After you were arrested in 1957 at Apalachin, were you not indicted and brought to trial in reference to the illegal Apalachin meeting of the Mafia?"

"Not only was I arrested but I was tried and convicted of having been at that meeting," Gianni said.

Stern looked pleased.

"However," Gianni continued, "the United States Circuit Court of Appeals overturned my conviction and threw that case out, indicating that there was no proof that anything illegal had occurred, that any crime had been committed. As far as I know, there wasn't anything illegal and there wasn't any crime committed, and I was not at any meeting of any Mafia, or any other organization that I know of in Apalachin in 1957, Mr. Stern."

Stern's smile vanished. He was stabbing at a piece of paper with a pencil. The other committee members were somber, watching Gianni.

"You know, Mr. Aquilino, you could be charged with perjury and sent to prison for not telling the truth before this committee?"

Gianni sat immobile, coolly, unblinkingly watching Stern. "If you think I'm committing perjury, Mr. Stern, you can take it to the court and try to convict me of it. And you can check with the Federal Appeals Court about Apalachin too. I'm telling the truth. Are you?"

Sandro leaned over to Gianni. "Please, Gianni, you're doing beautifully. But don't try to fence with him."

"I'm not the one being interrogated here, Mr. Aquilino," Stern said harshly.

Sandro leaned over to Gianni again. "Don't answer him, Gianni. Let it go."

Gianni sat waiting.

The entire room was motionless, silent.

"Well, this meeting you had in Apalachin, how did it come about?" asked Stern. "There must have been a plan far in advance so that everyone across the country would get together at this particular time?"

"I never knew and still don't know about any plan, Mr. Stern. At least for myself, I can say I was at home in Pawling and two friends drove up. They said they were going to Apalachin for a barbeque that day, and asked me to go along. I went. That's all there was to it as far as I'm concerned. I can't speak for the others you refer to across the country."

"Are you trying to say that nothing was planned, that it was just an accident that you happened to go there on that particular day with these two people?"

"That's right, Mr. Stern. Two old friends I hadn't seen in a long time."

"Who were these friends?" Stern asked sharply.

"Sal Angeletti and Vincent Tagliagambe," said Gianni.

"Was this Vincent Tagliagambe the boss of the same Cosa Nostra family you and Vito Giordano later headed?"

"Vincent Tagliagambe is dead four years," Gianni said. "He was deported nineteen years ago."

"Was he the boss of a family of the Cosa Nostra before being deported?" Stern repeated.

"Mr. Stern, as I said before, I'm not sure what you mean when you say the Cosa Nostra or the Mafia. If you define what you mean by Cosa Nostra or Mafia, I'll be able to answer your questions."

Stern studied Gianni. "The Cosa Nostra," Stern said slowly, sharply, "is an organization of criminals—a nationwide network of criminals—presided over by a commission to further a national criminal enterprise."

"Is this national organization and enterprise you're talking about centrally directed?" Gianni asked. "With a national plan of operation, a central budget? Things like that?"

"I'm not under examination, Mr. Aquilino," Stern spat out at Gianni.

"I'm only trying to find out what you're asking me, Mr. Stern. If I don't understand your question, how can I answer it?"

"Mr. Aquilino, you are obviously not telling the truth before this committee, you are obviously trying to insult this committee with your blatantly false answers." Stern was red in the face now.

Sandro leaned over to Gianni. "Let him talk. Don't get angry," Sandro said.

"What I'm saying is the truth, Mr. Stern. Is what you're saying the truth?" Gianni's voice had an edge to it.

Sandro leaned forward. "*Don't get angry, Gianni*—he'll shoot you down."

"Were you head of the same Mafia family after Tagliagambe was deported and before you were shot at?" Stern continued.

"I still would, respectfully, like to know exactly what you mean by Mafia," said Gianni.

"Was this Sal Angeletti a *capo* then, and is he now acting boss of the Mafia family of Vito Giordano?" Stern asked.

"What is a *capo*?" asked Gianni.

"What do you think it is?" Stern shot back.

Gianni shrugged, studied the desk momentarily, then looked up to Stern ingenuously. "Is it an Italian cop?"

Stern's eyes widened. He leaned back in his chair, staring down at Gianni. His eyes were hostile.

"Would the reporter read the last full question about Sal Angeletti to the witness," said Stern.

The reporter read aloud the question.

"Although you still won't, or perhaps can't, define it, Mr. Stern," said Gianni, "if you think the Mafia is a national organization, centrally directed and funded, there isn't any such thing. And what Sal Angeletti does is his own business. You ask him. If you want to know who I know, if I knew Vito Giordano, ask me."

"Did you know Vito Giordano?"

"Yes, since I was a kid on Mulberry Street. We used to play stickball together. I hit two sewers, Vito hit three."

The reporters were laughing now.

Stern was angered by that. "Is Rosario Gangi head of another family in the Mafia?" Stern demanded.

"I know Rosario Gangi too. We first met at dances in South

Brooklyn about fifty years ago. I've known him since then. However, as I've said, Mr. Stern, I know no nationwide organization involved in any national criminal scheme. If you mean something else, please tell me."

"We'll have a recess at this time," said Stern, rising abruptly.

The committee filed off the stage. Stern descended into the audience. Immediately he was swallowed up in a sea of reporters. He cut through them icily, walking directly to the witness table.

"Mr. Luca, this Aquilino—" Stern said menacingly, pointing his finger at Gianni.

"Don't point your finger at me, Mr. Stern," Gianni said. "I have respect for you. You should have respect for me."

Stern lowered his finger, returning to Sandro. "Your witness will be going up for perjury. The story he told us is ridiculous, and is obviously an attempt to get around answering questions in front of this committee by talking nonsense. I'm going to have him up on charges of perjury and contempt before you can even turn around. You hear that?"

Sandro nodded. "I heard you."

Stern turned toward Gianni. "Mr. Aquilino, your troubles have just begun. I'm going to break you. When these minutes are typed, you're going to jail."

"I've had troubles before. I can take them again, Mr. Stern."

12:30 P.M.

Gianni entered the garage. He was alone and tired, and he knew he had made an enemy who was, even now, planning to destroy him. And Gianni also knew that Stern and the F.B.I. could, if they wanted to, even frame him. But now he had to try to help Sal.

"Hiya, Gianni," said Angie the Kid.

"Hello, Kid."

Frankie the Pig was in the office eating peppers and eggs. A bottle of beer was on the desk. Gus was sitting by.

"Hello, Gianni," said Frankie the Pig. He cleared his things off the desk, so Gianni could take his place. He told him the news—that Big Diamond's boys had found the chocolate bunny and her boyfriend.

"How do they know he's the right one?" asked Gianni.

They told him and he nodded. "It's a good lead, anyway. It may be the right guy—and it may be nothing at all."

The others looked to Frankie the Pig.

"I sent Tony up there to grab the guy," said Frankie. "That way we'll know for sure, and we'll find out where the others are too."

Gianni studied Frankie the Pig. Before the boys had asked him to help, two nights ago, Gianni hadn't thought much about Frankie the Pig running across that lobby twelve years ago. Once in a while, after it first happened, he would wake up in the night, and he would see that face, twisted in bloodlust. But Frankie the Pig was older now, and the face was paunchy, had lost its youthful strength. It was no longer so fearsome.

"I don't think that was the right move," Gianni said flatly.

Frankie the Pig glanced around at the others, then back to Gianni. "Why not? If we've got the right guy, we can grab the rest of them too."

"I'm not sure we won't be better off if he's the wrong guy," said Gianni.

"What does that mean?"

"It means, simply, that if he's the right guy, and his friends find out we've got him, Sal's dead."

The others studied Frankie the Pig.

"I sent Tony and Lloyd and another colored guy. They're smart boys—they'll do it right," said Frankie.

"That's trusting to luck and I don't like that," said Gianni. "I make my own luck. When you hit, you should hit like lightning. Lightning only hits once, but if you figure it right, that's all you need."

As he spoke, Gianni was watching Frankie the Pig. Gianni was right on the line, he no longer had anything to lose—not with Frankie the Pig, not with anyone.

"I trust Tony," said Frankie.

"You better be able to," said Gianni.

"You want me to send somebody else up after them?"

Gianni shook his head. "I don't want you to do anything, Frankie."

The others were silent, looking from Gianni to Frankie the Pig.

"It's too late to worry about it now," said Gianni. "Besides, we have more important things to do."

"Like what?" said Frankie the Pig.

"We have to figure how to make sure they let Sal go alive after we pay the money," answered Gianni. "They're talking about getting the money—but how do we get our man back alive after that? I'm not leaving anything to luck, boys. We've got to prepare our lightning bolt now."

"Make them bring Sal with them, and exchange them," Gus suggested.

"They won't come that close," said Gianni. "They won't have Sal anywhere near us, and they won't come near us themselves. They'd be afraid that we'd grab Sal, and then kill them."

"Well, if we don't get close enough to see him, how can we know Sal's alive?" asked Bobby Matteawan.

"That's what we've got to figure out now," said Gianni. "We've got to find some way."

"How about—naw," said Angie the Kid.

"What is it, Angie?" said Gianni. "Every idea is good right now."

"I was thinking what if they brought him up on the Brooklyn Bridge or something like that, then we could watch him from below, maybe with binoculars? I've got a pair of binoculars. But, I guess that's not so good," Angie said diffidently.

"It's not bad, Angie," Gianni said. "The only thing is that they'd be with him. They could still kill him anyway before we got to him."

Angie looked at Gianni gratefully.

"We have to figure a way, then," said Frankie the Pig, "to be able to see him, and not have them with him?"

"That's right," said Gianni. "I don't know if we can do it."

"How about the subway, or the ferry," suggested Gus. "You know, they put him on one side and we wait on the other—they couldn't get at him then."

"How do we know they'll put him on after they're paid? And if they put him on before, why would we pay? Remember," said Gianni, "we have to figure out something they'll accept. And if we suggest anything that even smells like a trap, they'll tell us to stuff it."

"That makes it tough," said Bobby Matteawan. "Whatever we suggest is going to sound like a trap. I mean, how can we tell them where to bring Sal without it being a trap? They'll figure we know where it is and we'll have the place set up."

"Exactly," said Gianni. "They have to be secure, and we have to be secure, and they have to feel that we can't set them up. Otherwise, they won't go along with it."

"How the hell can you arrange something, and not know what it is?" asked Frankie.

Gianni rubbed his chin, and his hand slipped up along his face to his temple. "I'm going to think about it awhile," he said, rising. "First I'm going to catch about two hours sleep. I've been up all night. Then, we'll work something out. At least we'll try. Come on, Joey. Give me a ride."

"You're not going to Pawling, are you?" asked Frankie the Pig.

"No," said Gianni as he left.

7:45 P.M.

Again Gianni was seated at the desk in the garage. The telephone was right before him. He was rested; his nap had been a little longer than expected, but he felt much better. Now, showered and shaved, he looked straight ahead, thoughtful and anxious to get at it.

He lit another cigarette, doodling as he sat. The time was moving slowly toward the moment when his plan had to be sprung. Frankie the Pig came in and sat down next to him. Gianni did not speak. Frankie looked at his watch. "Five more minutes," he said.

"Right," said Gianni without turning.

The other men started coming in; they wanted to be where it was all going to happen.

"What about that plan to get Sal back safe?" asked Gus.

"You'll hear it first hand in a couple of minutes, Gus," said Gianni. "I'd rather go through it only once."

"Where the hell is Tony?" asked Joey. "We haven't heard from him since he went up there this morning."

Frankie the Pig said nothing.

"Maybe the niggers got him instead of the other way," said Bobby Matteawan.

The others fell silent now, watching Gianni, checking their watches. Gianni's mind was racing, probing his plan for defects.

8:00 P.M.

The phone rang.

"Hello," Gianni said.

"This is the time to start going," said Bull's deep voice on the other end. "You guys ready on your end?"

"We're ready to move," said Gianni. "Before you say anything about any plan of yours, I've got one of my own."

"You want to talk to your man. I know," said Bull. "I've got him right here."

"It's more than that," said Gianni. "I want to be sure he's still alive when the money is turned over."

"He'll be alive, man. Why should we kill him if you pay the money?"

"I've got a plan that'll help us both—you and me," said Gianni.

Gianni's men were leaning forward as they listened.

"Man, I'm not about to be sucked into some trap."

"It's no trap," Gianni said. "I think it covers you, and gives me a little more of an edge than you gave the guy you threw on our doorstep."

"Let's hear it," said Bull.

"You'll have to rent two cars with telephones," said Gianni.

"What? You kidding me, man?"

"No," said Gianni.

"Where am I going to get two cars with telephones, even if I wanted to?"

"Look it up in the phone book. You see, that's the beautiful part of it: you pick it yourself—I don't know where, I don't even want to know. I'm not trying to trap you. I just want some insurance."

"Yeah. What we supposed to do with the two cars?"

"You'll have some of your men in one car. Put Sal in the other car."

"By himself? You crazy, man. Why would you pay if we let him go first?"

"You won't let him go. You'll be right on top of him—your car right behind his. How can he get away?"

"Go ahead. It sounds too complicated already."

"That's all there is to it," said Gianni. "This way, Sal can telephone me here, and tell me he's in a car by himself. I'll tell my men to pay off. Your pickup man is in the car with the other phone. When he calls and tells you he's got the money, you let Sal drive away."

"Why do I want to go through all that trouble?" asked Bull.

"Because you want me to pay you the money. Even if you kill Sal, what is that worth to you? This is eighty-five thousand we're talking about. Eighty-five cash. That buys a lot of things. What do you want, the extra hundred bucks it costs for the cars? I'll send an extra hundred."

"It's not that, man. Don't be smart. Who needs it? I tell you it's no—you don't pay, I kill this old man."

"And then what will you have for all this? Nothing."

"But it's not as simple as that, man," said Bull. "I'm not going to tell you right now where to make the payoff. I'm not going to get trapped by nobody."

"I don't want to trap you. I've figured it out so nobody's trapping anybody. You get the cars wherever you want, drive anywhere you want, one car behind the other. How can you be trapped that way?" asked Gianni.

"Let me get this. We drive anywhere?"

"Right. Sal is in your hands, but not in your car. And we don't know where. We don't want to know. All I want to do is get my man back safe. He can drive home by himself when you drive away."

"I'm only going to give you the first stop now, so we can see if you're fucking around. When you get there, we'll call and tell you where to leave the money," said Bull. "How we going to do that with all this cat and mouse stuff?"

"That's easy," said Gianni. "Just be sure that your payoff place is near a phone. This way one of your men in the payoff car can be on the phone with you. When the others get the dough, they tell him and he tells you. You let Sal drive away. It's clean and simple. And we're not trying to trap you."

"Hold it," said Bull; "let's see: we got two cars with phones. Your old man gets in one. We get in another."

"Right," said Gianni.

"And we drive wherever we want—him up ahead, us behind?"

"Right."

"And then your old man calls you on the car phone and tells you he's in there by himself?"

"Right. Now he stays on the phone with me. After you tell my boys where to drop the money, they call me. I tell them it's okay to pay, because the old man's on the phone with me. And you get your money."

"And when our payoff man says he's got the money, we let your old man go."

"That's the whole thing. It's not so complicated," said Gianni.

"Yeah, man—and then right away you trace the cars and get to us. That's some big fly in the ointment."

"Are you telling me you can't rent the cars under some phony name? Why, you can steal them for all I care. How can we be fairer than that? You do what you want, where you want. All I want to know is that our man is alone, and you let him go."

"I guess we can do that. It'll take some time to get the cars," said Bull.

"How long?"

"Maybe a couple of hours. But remember, man, any funny business and your old man gets it from ear to ear."

"I know you mean it. That's why I worked it this way—you have control."

"Okay. It's 8:15 now. At 10:15 have one of your guys at the Woodhaven Lanes—that bowling alley in Queens. There ain't much traffic there, and it ain't got nothing around it, so we can see if you're trying to fuck around. Be there. Someone'll phone and tell you where to go and where to leave the money. They'll page Larry Fields. Have your guy answer to that name. And remember, man, don't think we're kidding."

The phone clicked. Gianni listened to the dead air for a moment.

"How can you be sure they'll let Sal go, even then?" asked Frankie the Pig.

"We can't be 100 percent sure, but at least he's got a running start. Sal was always a good wheel man. And remember, you don't want to fall in the cops' hands. The cops heard all this. They may stake the place out and follow you to the payoff. So shake them if they try it."

"Don't even worry about it," said Bobby Matteawan.

8:25 P.M.

Lieutenant Schmidt was on the phone. Feigin was standing next to him. Quinn had remained at the listening post in case anything else came in meanwhile.

"That's right, Woodhaven Lanes," Schmidt said into the phone. "Now get somebody over to the telephone company office and get a tap on all phones in that place. Make sure you get the public phones as well as the office phones." He listened to the voice on the other end.

"No, not just tapes. I want men on each of those taps for the next few hours. The call from the kidnapers will come in over the wires and we have to act on it immediately," said Schmidt. "We want to be in on the payoff if we can."

Schmidt listened again, looking at Feigin, his eyes inquiring if he had left anything out. Feigin shook his head.

"That's right. And as soon as the kidnapers call in, get word over Communications. We'll be nearby in private cars with squawk boxes."

The voice on the other end was talking again. Schmidt fished a cigarette out of a pack on the desk, cradled the phone under his chin and lit the cigarette, blowing the smoke out of the corner of his mouth.

"Okay, right," said Schmidt. "We'll be here a little while longer, then we're going out to that bowling alley."

He hung up and looked at Feigin. "Get Barrios to come with us. And tell Curtis he's coming too."

"Curtis? The young colored kid?" asked Feigin. "He's still wet behind the ears. What about Quinny?"

"We need someone on the wire here, and we need Curtis because he's probably the only detective Sal's boys don't know yet. He'll be able to go inside the bowling alley and hang around to see what's going on. The fact that he's colored makes it even better. Nobody will take him for a cop."

"Can't Barrios stay on the tape machine and let Quinn come with us?"

"You going to be lonely without your partner?"

"He's been in on this thing from the beginning. He knows the whole case," said Feigin.

"That's a good reason for him to stay on the wires," said the lieutenant. "But, okay, let Barrios take the wires, and Quinn can take one of the cars."

"Right, Lou. Are we going to alert some of the squads out there?" asked Feigin.

"No—the only thing they could do is fuck it up. We'll be at the bowling alley, and we'll get to the payoff at the same time Sal's people do. I'm afraid that more cars'll just endanger Sal even more. The way they got it set up, one word on the telephone to those goddamn cars, and they'll kill Sal."

"Yeah, how about that Aquilino? Two cars with phones—the whole works. Just like the movies," said Feigin.

"But it's good. It keeps us out of the picture and keeps them in, and yet lets Sal get a little breathing room. He's a clever bastard, that Aquilino."

"Can't we get those conversations on car phones by radio?" said Feigin.

"Yeah, have Communications set up their radios to pick up car phones—it's just like ship-to-shore. But I don't know what good it'll do. They could be anywhere. And by the time we got anything, they'd be someplace else." Schmidt waved his hand. "Have Communications try anyway."

"Okay."

"And let's move it. If we get out there now, we can set ourselves up and get a first-hand view of what's happening."

9:30 P.M.

Lieutenant Schmidt drove his station wagon into the large parking lot that surrounded the bowling alley. It was a square, windowless building; neon lights in the front blazed the name through the rainy night. Randolph Curtis, a young detective third grade, was sitting next to his lieutenant.

"There's Quinny's car," said Schmidt. He was looking straight ahead and could see the old red convertible with the black top that some punk vandal had sliced while the car was parked across from the station house. It was now parked on the far side of the bowling alley. Schmidt parked on the near side.

"I didn't see anybody in Quinn's car, lieutenant," said Curtis.

"They're in the back seat. Probably Feigin's jawing about turning in his papers."

Curtis smiled. He was eager, and pleased that the lieutenant had tapped him for this assignment.

Schmidt lifted the walkie-talkie from the seat beside him. "Stake Two, this is Stake One. Come in," Schmidt said into the small black speaker.

There was an abrupt squawk. "Stake One. This is Stake Two. In position," Feigin's voice replied.

"See anything?"

"Nothing. Only a nut would come bowling on a night like this," replied Feigin. "We're freezing our brass monkeys."

"Would you rather be nice and warm at home?" Schmidt asked him, smiling.

"Funny, Lou," said Feigin. "Here comes a car," he whispered in a quickened staccato. "It looks like—Matteawan's Cadillac. Sure, that's it."

"Anyone with him?"

"Looks like Frankie the Pig, and Angie," said Feigin. "They're parking about a hundred feet from us."

The wind gusted and rocked Schmidt's station wagon, fighting to get inside. The walkie-talkie gave a faint sound of static.

"They're looking around now," Feigin whispered into the walkie-talkie. "Matteawan and Frankie are getting out and moving toward the front door. Angie the Kid is coming over in your direction, Lou."

Curtis and Schmidt ducked low as they watched Angie the Kid walk to the corner of the building and study the parking lot. Then he retraced his steps.

"He's coming back your way," whispered Schmidt.

"Yeah. He's going inside now," said Feigin.

"Okay, now," Schmidt said to Curtis, "you go in there and mosey around. Just keep an eye on what's happening. Got your walkie-talkie?"

"Right here, lieutenant," Curtis said, tapping his trenchcoat pocket.

"Good," said Schmidt. "Take your coat off inside and put it down. If anything happens that we should know about, call me."

"Right."

"You have your gun with you?"

"Of course, lieutenant."

"I just want to be sure. These aren't kids in the street, Curtis—they're all killers. I'm not exaggerating to impress you. They really are. All of them."

"I'll take care of it all right, lieutenant."

"Sure you will. Go ahead."

Curtis got out of the car and started toward the bowling alley.

Gianni was sitting at his desk. He checked his watch and began to leaf through the newspaper on the desk for the third time. The phone rang.

"Hello?" said Gianni.

"*Ma, che cotz?*" gasped an exasperated Sal on the other end of the hollow-sounding connection. "Who's this? And what the hell's going on?"

"Hello, Sal. This is Gianni." He smiled.

"I should have recognized one of your hair-brained schemes. *Compard' ou me.* These niggers have me on a highway in the middle of the night talking on a goddamn phone. I don't even know where the hell I am."

"Are you alone, Sal?" Gianni asked.

"Yeah, but the bastards are right behind me."

"Are you all right?"

"Sure I'm all right," said Sal, "except that I haven't had a decent meal in four days. I keep thinking of those veal and peppers Maria was having for supper Monday. They must be cold by now."

Gianni laughed. "At least you're in good spirits. We're going to stay on this phone until the payoff and then you'll be on your own. Everything's under control."

"Gianni, with you on the job, what do I have to worry about? I knew you'd be out there. But I'd like to hit these bastards. When I get back, get me a gun. I'm going to find them by myself and kill them."

"Sal, this is short-wave radio. Everything you say is being broadcast. Be careful what you say. And right now I only want to know when they let you go. How many of them are there?"

"Two. Two big *tutzones*. The miserable bastards. What's supposed to happen now?"

"After we make the payoff, they'll let you drive away."

"You trust those no good bastards?" Sal asked.

"We have no choice. At least you're in a car by yourself," said Gianni.

"I ought to put on the brakes and let them crash into me."

"Sal, don't start going crazy," Gianni cautioned. "If they don't let you go, you can start doing things like that. Right now, let's play it straight."

"Whatever you say, *compard' ou me*."

Curtis walked casually into the bowling alley. It was a huge open place, with 35 lanes, side by side. About six lanes were being used. To the right was a snack bar. To the left was a supply shop which was now closed. Directly in front of Curtis was a counter with a man seated at a cash register.

"Bowl?" the man asked.

"Not right now," replied Curtis. He walked to the left, where the active lanes were. Behind the alleys were three rows of spectator seats. Curtis stood behind them, watching a black ball drone down alley 3, crashing for a 7-10 split. He could feel Frankie the Pig and Bobby Matteawan staring at him from alley 5. Angie the Kid was getting set to roll.

"Maybe that's one of the niggers?" Bobby Matteawan whispered to Frankie the Pig.

"I just wish I knew," Frankie the Pig whispered. "I'd strangle the son of a bitch right here."

"There's another nigger bowling by himself on alley 3. Maybe he's another one," said Matteawan.

There was a crash of pins. "Hey, I got a strike, I got a strike," Angie the Kid exulted, hopping back to the scoring table.

"Fuck the strike, Kid. Keep bowling," said Frankie the Pig.

"But I just did. It's your turn," said Angie the Kid.

"Yeah, maybe you'd better, Frankie," said Bobby Matteawan.

"No, you go next," Frankie the Pig said. "I don't even know how. Besides, I want to watch those niggers."

Curtis noticed the colored man bowling by himself in lane 3. He wanted to get out from under the eyes of Frankie the Pig. He moved down toward lane 3.

"Hey, how you doin'?" asked Hartley, seeing Curtis standing behind him. He was glad for a little cover himself.

"How you doin'?" replied Curtis. "You got a game?"

"No," replied Hartley. "I'm just throwing a few balls. Want to join me?"

"Sure," said Curtis. He walked up to the main desk and rented a pair of shoes. He went back to lane 3 and put them on.

By this time Frankie the Pig was moving awkwardly toward the foul line, the bowling ball dangling heavily from his three fingers. He lumbered across the line and released it. It traveled through the air halfway down the alley and landed with a crunch on the polished wood.

"Alley 5," said the main desk over the loudspeakers. "A little easier on the woodwork, please."

"*A fongool*," said Frankie the Pig, walking back to the bench, giving the main desk a deadly side glance.

"Hey, you've got another turn, Frankie," said Angie the Kid.

"Stuff it up in your ass," said Frankie as he sat down.

"I'm Frank Smith," Hartley said, shaking Curtis' hand.

"Burton Shaw," Curtis replied. He began trying his fingers in the bowling balls on the rack behind him.

Hartley rolled a ball and took down all but one pin.

"Nice shot," said Curtis walking forward.

"Thanks," said Hartley. "You from around here?"

"No, Long Island City. I was supposed to meet some guys here," said Curtis. "But I don't see them." He noticed that Hartley was carefully watching Frankie the Pig and the others. Hartley took down the other pin with the second ball. Curtis bowled a six on his first ball. His second ball took down one more.

"How the hell long do I have to keep driving?" Sal complained into the phone.

"*Pazienza, compard*," said Gianni, "it won't be long until the payoff, then you'll be free."

"I think we're in Long Island somewhere, but I'm not sure," said Sal.

"They still behind you?"

"Right on my ass."

A phone began to ring behind them. Frankie the Pig leaped up. The phone kept ringing. The man from the main desk started toward the three booths. So did Frankie the Pig. Frankie made it first. But none of those phones was ringing—Frankie the Pig could still hear the sound coming from somewhere in back. The man from the main desk pushed open the door of the men's room. The phone stopped ringing. The man came out.

"Is there a Larry Fields here?" he called out.

"Yeah, that's for me," said Frankie the Pig. He rushed into the men's room. The phone was on the wall, the receiver dangling, making a slow circle through the air. Frankie snared it.

"Hello?"

"You ready to move?" asked Bull.

"Ready." Frankie's lips curled in hate.

"This isn't the same voice," said Bull.

"No. I'm making the payoff. He sent me," said Frankie the Pig.

"Okay. Now get it straight the first time. You ready?"

"Come on, come on," said Frankie the Pig. "Let's not waste time."

"Okay then, listen." Bull spoke and Frankie the Pig listened.

Curtis had watched Frankie the Pig go into the men's room to get the call. He wasn't sure Communications had tapped that number. Even if they had, he thought he'd better get back to Schmidt and be ready to move. This was coming off right now.

"I think I'm going to split," said Curtis, turning to Hartley. "I'm going to try to find those cats that were supposed to meet me."

"Okay, thanks for the game," said Hartley. He too was watching the men's room door.

Curtis took off the bowling shoes, put on his own and moved as quickly as he could without attracting notice.

"Here comes Curtis," Feigin's voice squawked through the walkie-talkie.

"I got him," said Schmidt.

Curtis moved quickly to the station wagon and got inside. "The call is coming in over the men's room phone."

"Shit," said Schmidt. "Stake One to headquarters, Stake One to headquarters, do you read me?"

"We read you," the box squawked with a great deal of static. Schmidt turned up the squelch button.

"Anything from Communications yet?" Schmidt asked.

"Hold on," said the voice at the local precinct house. There was a long pause. "Nope, nothing coming through on any of the tapped phones. I just called them."

Schmidt frowned. "We won't need any radio patrol cars then. We'll have to play it by ear from here."

"Roger," said the voice from the precinct.

"You get that, Stake Two?" Schmidt asked.

"We're listening," said Feigin.

"Have they come out yet?"

"Not yet. We're watching."

The wall phone rang in the garage. Joey picked it up. "Hello? It's Frankie the Pig, Gianni," Joey told him; "he's got the place for the pay-off. He wants to know if it's all right to go to make the payoff."

"You still okay, Sal?" Gianni asked into the other phone.

"Okay, but hurry up, for Christ's sake," said Sal. "I'll be in Palermo soon."

Gianni laughed. "Ask Frankie where he has to make the payoff," he said to Joey.

Joey spoke into the wall phone, then turned to Gianni. "Woodlawn Cemetery."

Gianni nodded slowly. "Tell Frankie it's okay to go."

"Here they come now," Feigin's voice squawked softly.

"Don't follow them too obviously," cautioned the lieutenant.

"How the hell can you follow anybody in this godforsaken area without them knowing it," said Feigin. "No wonder they picked it. There they go."

Bobby Matteawan's car screamed across the parking lot and into the night. Schmidt floored his accelerator.

"Take the squawk box and tell Feigin to hustle it up," Schmidt said to Curtis.

The two private cars with police raced out of the parking lot and onto the city streets. Bobby Matteawan made a left turn a block ahead. Schmidt was first to get to the corner. He reached the turn in time to catch sight of Matteawan making another right.

"The son of a bitch is trying to ditch us," said Schmidt. "He knows we're back here."

"Hello, mobile operator, did you get through to my number yet?" Bull asked. He was on the far side of Woodlawn Cemetery in a phone booth. His car was parked near a gate, the motor running.

"I am trying, sir. I can't seem to get a circuit right now. Do you want to place your call later?"

"No, I want to place it now. It's an emergency," said Bull. "I've got to get a call through to that car."

"I'm sorry, there are only a few circuits, sir," said the mobile operator.

"Just get me one, will you, baby. I have to get that car."

"Sir, I can't just cut in on anybody, can I?"

Bull drew in his breath. She was a sister, so he couldn't very well dress her down. "No, I guess you can't. I'll hold on."

"I have other calls to make, sir. You hold on by yourself. I'll come back." The phone went dead.

"That's a nigger bitch," Bull muttered as he held the phone to his ear. He looked toward where Alfred would appear after he got the money.

"Come on, Bobby, you're losing those bastards," said Frankie the Pig, looking out the rear window. Schmidt's car hadn't even turned the last corner as Bobby Matteawan threw his car into a four-wheel drift and gunned around another left turn.

"They aren't going to follow us nowhere," said Bobby Matteawan, his face tense as he watched every object hurtling up in front of them. They screamed on through the dark.

"Alert the precinct," Schmidt told Curtis. "Use the walkie-talkie. See if any prowl cars can see this crazy bastard in front of us."

Curtis spoke to the precinct.

"Okay, we'll put out a bulletin," squawked the box.

"No, for Christ's sake," screamed Schmidt. "Tell them just to try and watch where the hell the car is headed."

Curtis repeated the message.

"Roger," said the precinct. "One of our cars just spotted them. They're headed west, back to New York."

Schmidt turned left and headed in that direction.

"I can place your call now," the operator said to Bull.

"Thank you, operator," Bull said through clenched teeth. He heard the ringing at the other end. It was a funny buzz of a ring.

"Hello?" said Yank's voice, faint and streaked with static.

"It's me," said Bull. "Everything okay?"

"Me and Duck're right behind him," Yank replied.

"Okay here too," said Bull. "I'm waiting for Momma to show. Hang on till he arrives."

"Yeah, Momma," said Yank.

"You hold now, and we'll keep this thing open," said Bull. "It's tough getting through to you.

"Okay."

Bobby Matteawan turned left onto the overpass, crossing the highway to New York, and turned left again. He was next to the cemetery. There were no streetlights nearby. The place was as silent as tombs usually are. The wind was whistling cold and wet across the frozen trees. As far as they could see, the entire cemetery was surrounded by a ten-foot stone and cement wall.

"What a place this guy picks," said Frankie the Pig, surveying the wall. "Who the hell could even get over that wall? And if you got to the top, they'd kill you before you hit the ground."

"What do we do now?" asked Bobby Matteawan.

"We go slow until we see a white cloth over the wall. Then we just throw the money over."

Matteawan drove slowly along the curb while Frankie the Pig and Angie the Kid watched the wall. Frankie said, "Shut off your lights."

Bobby Matteawan shut the lights and continued slowly.

"There it is," said Angie the Kid. Over the wall, apparently suspended by a rope, a white handkerchief was bobbing.

"Stop the car," said Frankie the Pig. He got out and studied the handkerchief, then the wall above. It was solid stone and cement, without an opening anywhere in sight.

"You there, you black cocksucker?" he shouted into the wind.

"Just throw that bread over, you white motherfucker," shouted Alfred, from the other side.

"I'd cut you open with a knife and shit in your chest, you lousy black bastard," Frankie shouted.

"I ain't got all day," Alfred replied. "Throw that stuff, or I'll do the same to that old man of yours."

Frankie heaved the money bag over the wall. He watched it sail out of view, then heard movement on the other side. The car behind him moved quickly onto the sidewalk and pulled up directly next to the wall. Matteawan and Angie were out in a moment, jumping onto the hood and then the roof. Frankie the Pig leaped up beside them. Their heads didn't even reach the top of the wall. Bobby Matteawan jumped up and pulled himself to the top of the wall.

"I can't see a goddamn thing," Bobby Matteawan said.

"Okay. What are you guys doing up there?" Lieutenant Schmidt said from behind them. Flashlights shone on the three men standing on the roof of the car. Quinn pulled up directly behind Schmidt's car. Feigin flashed a third light on the three men standing stock still on the car roof.

"I come to see my mother's grave," said Bobby Matteawan, "may she rest in peace."

Suddenly a roar of a belly laugh burst from Feigin. Quinn joined him. Schmidt looked over at his two detectives, then back at the three goons looking foolish on top of the car. He began to laugh and turned out his flashlight.

Bull was still holding the phone, talking to Yank. He heard a noise, and then footsteps. He saw Alfred squeezing through the bars of the gate.

"You got it, man?" asked Bull.

"I got something," he said, bringing over the wrapped paper bag. In the light of the booth he tore off the wrapping. Inside were bundles of cash.

"Count it," said Bull.

Alfred took the money out, and together they counted it, putting the packages back in the bag as they did so.

"Eighty-five thousand." Alfred said admiringly.

"Let me look at it," said Bull. He fanned through the money, looking at selected bills.

"Looks real to me," said Alfred.

"It is," said Bull. "Okay, baby, we got it," he said into the phone.

"Let him go?" asked Yank.

"Let him go. See you later," replied Bull.

"Okay."

Alfred got into the car as Bull slid behind the wheel. They moved out quickly, disappearing into the dark quiet streets of Queens.

"Hey, Gianni, these guys just flashed their lights at me," Sal said into the phone.

"What are they doing?" asked Gianni.

"It looks like they're dropping off. Yeah—they're dropping off me," Sal said. "They've just shot off the highway on an exit. They're gone. The bastards are gone!"

"Come on home, *compard' ou me.*"

"With pleasure," said Sal. "But how the hell do I get home when I don't know where I am?"

11:15 P.M.

Gianni lifted his Scotch and water. Frankie the Pig had just proposed a toast. Gus, Joey, Bobby Matteawan and Angie the Kid were exuberant now, drinking to take the edge off the tension and fear that had hung over them for four long days.

The garage door suddenly opened and Sal walked in. He stood in the center of the floor, blinking, smiling, hardly believing that it was truly over.

Joey saw him first. "Boss," he cried, running over. He embraced Sal, kissing his cheek.

The others came around joyously, slapping his back, shaking his hand.

Sal looked at Gianni. Gianni stood there laughing softly. They moved toward each other, their faces glowing, and embraced.

"I didn't think we'd get you back, *compard' ou me*," said Gianni.

"What the hell are you talking about?" said Sal, holding him at arm's length, looking into Gianni's eyes. "You think those bastards could compete with you, *compard'*? I wasn't worried. I tell you the truth, though"—Sal turned toward the others, his arm still around Gianni's shoulders—"when they put me in that car tonight, I wasn't so sure I wasn't going for a ride. But when the guy with me got out—my God, I said to myself, look what this Silver Eagle can get these bastards to do. He got out of the car, and left me alone! But you know they left me at the ass end of the world? I had to ask a cop how to get the hell out of there. You believe it? I was out in the middle of nothing. You did well, my friend," Sal turned to Gianni again. "*Dio mio*, you're a genius." Sal kissed Gianni on both cheeks.

"Where's a drink?" said Sal, turning. "Everybody's celebrating except me!"

"Here, boss," said Joey eagerly, pouring a tumbler of neat Scotch.

"Stop! Do you want to kill me?"

"To Gianni," he said, raising his glass. "I owe you my life, *compard'*."

"We're even," said Gianni.

"Come on, drink hearty," said Sal.

Suddenly Sal looked worried. "What about my wife?" he asked Gianni.

"She's all right. I told her you had to go out of town for a couple of days."

"I can just hear her bitching now," said Sal. "She'll want to know why I didn't take her with me. I'm supposed to be a tough guy—how come I have to listen to that?"

"Tell her next time you're kidnaped you'll take her along," said Gianni. They laughed.

Suddenly Sal turned deadly serious. "Now, let's go find those bastards and get our money back. You know who they are?"

"Big Diamond located a man they think is connected with this," said Frankie the Pig. "I sent Tony out to bring him in this afternoon. I haven't heard from Tony at all—we're afraid they got him."

"They didn't get him," said Gianni, his humor gone now. He put down his drink, looking at Frankie the Pig, then at Sal. "Frankie sent Tony up to Harlem to grab this man; that's true, Sal. However, I believe that if his friends had found him missing, right in the middle of negotiations, they'd have panicked or exploded. Either way, I believe it would have triggered their killing you."

"Lucky Tony didn't get him, then," said Sal.

"Yeah, what the hell, it all worked out," said Frankie the Pig, relieved.

"It's not as easy as that." Gianni was staring at Frankie the Pig.

The others fell silent, aware that something was going on.

"It didn't just work out by chance," said Gianni. "I told you I don't trust in luck. Tony came to see me at the hearing today instead of going up to Harlem with Lloyd."

All eyes turned to Frankie the Pig, then to Sal.

"Tony told me what you wanted him to do," said Gianni. "He also told me that he didn't like the idea and he wanted me to know about it before he went ahead."

"Why that little weasel," said Frankie the Pig. "When I give him an order—"

"Hold it, let me hear this," said Sal, raising his hand.

"I told Tony to go up to Harlem and just watch this Alfred," said Gianni. "I told him to try to find out if he was really in on it, and to stay out of sight. I haven't heard from him yet, but I know the colored guys didn't get him."

"If they had, I'd be dead by now," said Sal. He looked at Frankie. The office phone rang. Joey took the call. "It's Tony. He wants you, Gianni."

"No, he wants Sal," Gianni replied.

Sal took the phone. "Tony? I hear you did fine work. Really fine, I appreciate it. Where are you now?"

"I got them. Lloyd and I've been watching these creeps all day. We even saw you and followed you on the road tonight. We kept about a half-mile back—saw the whole thing."

"You mean, you were right there with me?" asked Sal. "Why didn't you take the bastards?"

"Because I wanted you to get out first."

"Where were you after they went away?"

"I followed them. I wanted to get them all together again. And now they're all celebrating."

"You've got them now?" asked Sal.

"Yes," Tony replied.

"Where are they?" Sal asked hungrily.

"In the Black Pussy Café on St. Nicholas Avenue and 139th Street."

"Keep the bastards there, Tony. You keep them there," said Sal. He hung up the phone and stormed out of the office.

"Let's go. Get some of your boys, get the guns, get ropes and weights." He was looking around the garage, trying to find anything to use to crack across a skull. "Get your toughest boys together—Gus, Bobby. And some baseball bats. I want to do a job on their heads personally."

"Let's go," said Frankie the Pig, pulling out an automatic from his waistband, sliding its bolt to arm it.

"No, you stay here where you can't fuck things up," Sal said curtly.

Frankie the Pig looked at him in amazement. "What do you mean?"

"What the hell do you think I mean?"

"I'm the underboss, I'm second in command," Frankie the Pig protested.

"And when you found yourself really on your own," said Sal, "you almost got me killed because of that goddamn temper—because you don't think. Tony, now, he thinks. Look at the good work he's done."

Gianni watched the scene with a certain pleasure. The other men looked at Sal, then moved slowly away from Frankie the Pig.

"You demoting me, Sal?"

"Right. Demotion. You're out, Tony's in. As of right now. You want to stay on with us, or you want to go someplace else?" Sal's eyes were cold and hard.

"Go where?"

"That's up to you," said Sal.

"I know where the someplace else is," said Frankie the Pig. He looked around him. The others watched dispassionately. "I'm staying."

"No funny business," said Sal. "Any funny business and you'll be lying all over the street the way those niggers are going to be lying all over the street in a few minutes. They're going to be dead."

"They're already dead," said Bobby Matteawan.

Gianni turned to Sal. "No!"

"What do you mean, *compard'*?" asked Sal. "We've got these niggers now. We have to teach them a lesson, don't we?"

"I agree," said Gianni. "But you don't have to kill them, Sal."

"Don't kill them? You want me to give them a medal, a hug? You know better than that, Gianni. They got to be taught they can't fuck around with us—nobody can."

"That's all right. Just don't kill them. You said you owe me something. This is what I'm asking you."

"What do you want me to do with them then?"

"Throw the place out in the street, fine—hit them with bats, teach them a lesson. Look: The worst thing you can do to them is take their money and their rackets; let everyone know they're marked men, tie a can to their tails, so no one will do business with them. Just don't kill them," Gianni repeated. "I don't want any more blood on my conscience. I tracked them down, I got you back. I don't want their blood."

"Give them a beating and leave them alone? You getting soft in the head, *compard'*?" Sal asked.

Gianni looked at him steadily. Then he smiled. "Besides," he said, "I've got a better way for you to take care of them for good without killing them."

"It's got to be crazy," said Sal, "but I'd better listen."

Gianni said, "After you really give them their lumps, toss them over to the cops. After all, they killed a guy—and the cops have them admitting it on that phone of ours they tapped. Let the cops put them away for you."

Sal studied Gianni a moment longer. "That head of yours never stops, *compard' ou me.* Cops." Finally he shook his head. "I never let cops do anything for me, Gianni. You know that."

Gianni sighed and just perceptibly lifted his shoulders.

Sal nodded toward the outside and the cars. The others moved out. Sal followed. Then turned: "You come too, demoted wise guy," he said to Frankie the Pig.

Gianni went into the office and put on his overcoat. Joey came into the garage as Gianni was walking to the doorway.

"Sal sent me back to drive you home," said Joey.

"Okay, Joey. All of a sudden I'm tired."

They went outside and got into Gianni's silver Cadillac. Joey got behind the wheel and started away from the curb.

FRIDAY, FEBRUARY 12

1:00 A.M.

THREE CARS PULLED UP in front of the Black Pussy Café. On the way up, a car with five of Gus's boys had joined them. Tony and Lloyd got out of a car in the shadows.

"Hello, Tony," said Sal, happy for a moment.

"I'm glad to see you," said Tony, shaking his hand. "I'm sure glad to see you. This is Lloyd—a real good guy."

Sal shook hands with Lloyd. "They still in there?" he asked.

"Yeah. They're having drinks, getting a little stoned," said Lloyd.

"Where are they sitting?"

"Third booth back, on the left," replied Tony.

"Good. Let me go in alone," said Sal. "Have a couple of guys watch the back entrance."

"I already did, Sal," said Gus.

Sal opened the front door and walked up to the bar. He was the only white man in the place. The bartender noticed him first, then a couple of customers sitting at the bar looked over.

"How about a drink?" Sal said loudly, slapping his hand on the bar.

Alfred looked up and saw Sal. He nudged Yank. Soon all five men seated at the table and the five women with them were watching Sal.

The rest of the customers at the bar and at the tables fell silent; something was in the air.

Sal downed a shot of Scotch neat. He did not look toward the back. He tossed a five dollar bill on the bar.

The five men in the back began to slide out from their table. Bull reached down for the attache case full of money that was next to his chair.

The only sound in the place was the clicking of the jukebox automatically seeking out the next selection.

Sal turned now. He looked right at the table where the five men were seated. "Hiya Bull," he said, his eyes fierce.

Bull stood in place, staring back at Sal. He said nothing. His eyes moved toward the front door as it opened.

Frankie the Pig, Gus, Bobby Matteawan, Angie the Kid, Louie the Animal, and Tony entered. Two of Gus's boys—real hard-rock types—entered with them. One sat at the bar. The other sat at the first table. They each took out a pistol and held it down flat before them. The patrons—except those at Bull's table—started to scramble toward the rear.

"Move slow," ordered Sal loudly. "Have somebody watch for cops," he said to his men.

"Right, Sal," said Gus.

"Listen mister, we don't want any trouble," said the bartender.

"Forget it; you got it," said Sal. He turned toward the back. "How about handing over that case." He nodded toward the attaché case.

The girls sitting with Bull and his bunch got up from the table and moved to the rear of the place with the other customers. There were about twenty people, all standing, silently watching.

Tony waved the bartender to the rear with them. The bartender raised his hands and moved quietly. Tony walked over to Bull and kicked his chair to the floor. He pulled the attaché case roughly from his hands and gave it to Angie the Kid. Angie handed it to Sal. Tony nodded to Gus's men. They trained their pistols on the five colored men as Tony frisked them one at a time. He relieved them of six pistols and five knives.

Sal opened the attache case and counted. "A hundred eighty thousand." He looked up. "A hundred eighty. We just made up our vig, Tony. That's the first step. Next."

Tony looked at Sal, then Frankie the Pig, then the others. They started moving toward Bull.

"Anybody else in the back there want trouble?" asked Tony.

Nobody moved. One gun was thrown from the crowd to the floor. Angie the Kid picked it up and put it on the table with the rest of the gathered weapons. Gus's man was minding them.

Tony turned and took a baseball bat from Bobby Matteawan. He walked slowly toward Bull, his eyes like coals, fixed on him. Bull raised his hands, bracing himself for battle. Tony took a cut with the bat swinging full as if for a fastball—Bull's middle was the ball. Bull raised his hands to grab for the bat, but Tony had sent it in too hard. It crashed through Bull's hands and dug hard into his gut. Bull moaned as he folded to his knees.

Frankie the Pig walked up quickly and lifted Hartley by the shirt-front. He started screaming as Frankie the Pig lifted him into the air. "Man, I didn't do nothing, I didn't do nothing," Hartley squealed.

"You went bowling tonight," said Frankie the Pig, "and I don't like bowling." He lifted Hartley bodily and looked around for a place to throw him. Yank moved from the table to grab Frankie the Pig. Bobby Matteawan sprinted up and leaped through the air across a table onto Yank.

Frankie the Pig lumbered toward the bar with Hartley over his head. He threw him over the bar, hurling him into the bottles and the glasses lined neatly at the rear. Hartley screamed as he crashed. He landed behind the bar as glass and mirrors and broken whiskey bottles kept cascading upon him.

Bull was on his knees, reaching for the wall, trying to rise. Tony brought the bat down on top of his head. It sounded like Cookie Lavagetto connecting for that ninth-inning double against the Yankees. Bull went down, full out.

Bobby Matteawan had taken Yank down with him. Yank grabbed him and wrestled Matteawan to the ground. Matteawan struggled to get his hands on Yank's throat as Yank sailed a couple of good punches into his face.

Frankie the Pig waded into Duck. He grabbed him by his lapels and jerked him forward, lowering his own head as he pulled him. Duck's face mashed against the bone on the top of Frankie the Pig's head. His nose broke and two teeth came out instantly. Frankie the Pig rammed Duck backwards into the wall.

Angie the Kid steered around Frankie the Pig, who was now pummeling Duck's stomach. He gave Yank, who was sitting on Bobby Matteawan's chest, a vicious kick in the back. Yank screamed and reached for his back. Matteawan laughed evilly and reached for Yank's throat.

Gus had moved on Alfred. Alfred pulled a knife from his leg and started to circle. He didn't see Tony, a .400 hitter for sure. Tony swung for the seats on a low inside pitch. He took Alfred right at the knees. Alfred screamed, falling backwards onto his rump in the crowd. The crowd scrambled away. Gus ran over and grabbed Alfred, lifting him up. With his free hand, he punched him quickly in the stomach, then gave him a right hook, and a follow-up straight to the mouth. Alfred was out.

Frankie the Pig now had Duck against the wall in a headlock. He squeezed him until Duck let go of his waist. Frankie the Pig twisted Duck around, picked him up over his shoulder and began running toward the front of the bar. Sal and the others moved out of the way as Frankie the Pig wound up like a javelin thrower and heaved Duck through the front window out into the street. The front window, the neon tubing, the curtains, all crashed out into the street with him.

Bobby Matteawan was on top of Yank now. He pulled a cleaver out of his waistband. Laughing, he lifted the cleaver over his head, ready to split Yank's skull in half. He started his forward swing as Yank, paralyzed, watched the glitter of razor-sharp steel start to descend.

"Stop, Bobby!" commanded Sal. He was still standing with the attache case in his arms.

Bobby Matteawan heard his master's voice and stopped, turning around. His free hand instinctively went to Yank's throat, so he would know where his prey was while he was distracted.

"Don't kill him," said Sal.

Bobby rose backward, standing over Yank, the cleaver hanging motionlessly at his side, his fingers twitching on its handle. Yank rose to his knees slowly, moving to get up. Matteawan dropped the cleaver to the floor. It was right in front of Yank's hands. Yank moved suddenly toward it. Matteawan reached for a chair he knew was right next to him, hoisted it overhead, and with a gleeful scream, let it come down on Yank's head with all his force. Yank sank to the floor in a crumpled heap.

"Throw this joint out in the street," Sal ordered.

"We didn't do nothing, mister," the bartender said from the rear.

"This'll keep you from ever thinking about it," said Sal. "Wreck the joint. Get these bums into the cars," he said, pointing at Bull and the other four. "Put them in the trunks."

He turned to the others. Tony was already at work, splintering chairs on top of tables. Angie the Kid swept the shelves of glasses and bottles. He then threw a chair through whatever mirrors were not already broken. Bobby Matteawan was heaving furniture through the side windows. Gus was breaking the tables against the walls.

"Wreck this lousy joint," Sal demanded, his fury reaching a crescendo. He kicked at a table. "Ouch, my corn, *Putana*," he howled.

The bar was in a shambles. The people in the rear nervously pressed back, shifting around so as not to get in the way, watching every usable piece of furniture, everything in the place, being pulverized and thrown into the street.

"Come on, we've got more work to do," said Sal, satisfied finally that the place was wrecked. "Let's get out of here."

Gus was in front with his boys, shoving the battered kidnapers into the trunks of the three cars.

"Keep your hands off, white bastard," Bull hurled out as they pushed him over the rear bumper of Matteawan's car.

"Get in there you punk, or I'll split that rock you call a head," Matteawan said, slapping the flat side of the cleaver against Bull's back.

"Why are we putting them in the trunk?" one of Gus's boys asked him.

"Sal wants it that way, that's all," Gus answered. "He's got something on his mind."

"This ain't the end man, this is the beginning," said Bull as they began to close the trunk lid down on him. "We ain't finished, man."

"You're shit, man," Matteawan mimicked, pushing his hand in Bull's face, shoving him back, then slamming down the lid on top of him.

The contagion vanished as quickly as it had come, leaving the people in the bar staring at each other in disbelief.

11:00 A.M.

Gianni was seated in his glass-enclosed sunroom, which faced south. In the pond, at the foot of the sloping hill on which his stone house stood, a swan was slowly preening its feathers. The warm sun shone in softly; the astronauts were safe and in isolation. Gianni was dressed in slacks and a shirt open at the neck. He was reading the *Times* over a cup of cappucino.

The phone rang. His mind immediately jumped back to the events of the night before.

"It's Mr. Luca," said Louisa, the housekeeper.

Gianni got up and went to the phone.

"Good morning, Sandro."

"Hello, Gianni. Did you see the *Times* this morning?"

"I'm reading it now, but we only get the early edition up here. What's in it?"

"Well, there's a big report on your hearings."

"That figures."

"The reporters got a big kick out of your answers. They didn't believe your testimony, but they apparently enjoyed your giving Stern a rough time."

"I did too, though I'm sure he didn't," said Gianni. "You think he'll try to get me for perjury or contempt?"

"Gianni, I told you: you can't be in contempt if you answer. And as for perjury, you didn't lie about anything."

"Okay," Gianni said. "You're the lawyer."

"And you know, a strange thing happened last night in the Elizabeth Street precinct," Sandro continued.

"What was that?"

"The *Times* says some unknown people threw five very beat-up but live colored men onto the steps of the precinct house about one o'clock this morning. And it just so happens that those five men are wanted on kidnaping and murder charges in the Bronx. They were all booked and are being arraigned this morning."

Gianni smiled.